SAM CRESCENT

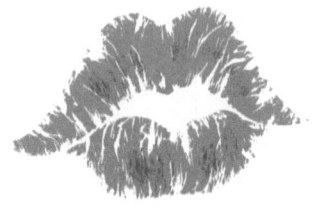

EVERNIGHT PUBLISHING ®

www.evernightpublishing.com

Copyright© 2020

Sam Crescent

Editor: Karyn White

Cover Artist: Sour Cherry Designs

Jacket Design: Jay Aheer

ISBN: 978-0-3695-0204-9

SAM CRESCENT

DEDICATION

I want to say a big thank you to my readers. Your constant support of Chaos Bleeds and The Skulls make sure I continue to write their stories.

Without Evernight and my editor Karyn White, Blind Devotion wouldn't have become the story it has. Thank you so much to all of you.

SAM CRESCENT

BLIND DEVOTION

Chaos Bleeds, 4

Sam Crescent

Copyright © 2014

Prologue

As he sat in Devil's office, Pussy didn't know why he'd been called to the president of Chaos Bleeds. Most of the time he was in this office for a meeting with the other men in the club, not one on one. Within a month of dealing with him, Frederick Gonzalez had changed the game, and now they were all in turmoil. The Skulls were no longer out of the danger zone. Tiny had had to make a deal with Gonzalez to get back Butch's woman back. Pussy felt for the club. They all did. Gonzalez was proving to be a bigger problem than even he anticipated. So much had happened in the last few months, and Pussy was struggling to keep up. Their last visit to The Skulls had been around the revelation of Alex being a father. He joked about the trouble The Skulls were attracted to, but Pussy really wished for a break. Chaos Bleeds were starting to get problems at their door as well. This time it seemed the two MCs had the same problem to deal with.

Their deliveries and rides were more dangerous

than ever before, all because of their deal with Gonzalez on transporting drugs. Pussy hated going on the runs with his brothers. Being on his bike was the fun part, but the danger, the risk, wasn't fun. The chance of them getting caught was stronger than ever. There was no way they could transport over thirty girls without someone finding out the truth. The deal with no girls had soon changed. Devil couldn't refuse as their hands were tied. They all knew who the real boss was at the moment, and it wasn't the president of their club.

The fun of settling down was now turning into a nightmare. Moving around, never sticking to the same patch of land, had kept them away from greedy bastards. They were in danger of going to prison or worse, ending six feet fucking under. Pussy liked living, as did the other members in the club.

"What can I do for you, boss?" Pussy asked, sitting into the chair. Staring at a picture on the far wall of Lexie and Devil had him thinking about Sasha Carmichael. Ever since their encounter over a month ago he couldn't get her out of his mind. When he went to the diner he saw her sitting on her own looking petrified. He made a point of talking to her even though her stepfather hated him. Pussy didn't give a fuck what others thought of him. The club mattered to him more than his own personal feelings.

Running a hand through his hair, he forced himself to look away from the photograph. His president, Devil, was one lucky man, and all of the brothers were happy for him and Lexie.

"The Skulls are now part of the shit. They received a head yesterday with one of Butch's old friends. Her head was inside a box sent to Butch's woman. Gonzalez has stepped up the game." Devil was frowning as he spoke.

"Okay, boss, you're starting to scare me, and I don't scare easily." Pussy sat up and then leaned over, resting his elbows on his knees. He knew that Gonzalez was threatening their lives at every turn. A simple business deal to keep Curse alive had suddenly turned into a fucking nightmare. Pussy, for one, was tired of being the lapdog of someone he hated. Gonzalez wasn't a good man, not even a decent man, and yet Ashley was still alive, which surprised him. "Was the woman a friend?"

"No, the woman helped Butch escape Daddy Gonzalez when the kid was thirteen." Devil ran a hand over his face. "Before I show you what I'm about to show you. I want you to know that I never intended for this to happen."

Standing up, Pussy waited for Devil to peel away the box. The moment he saw the severed head and recognized the hair, Pussy gripped his stomach. *Fuck*. He'd never been in love with Ashley. They were never going to get married, have a load of kids, and be happy. She was one of his best friends, the only female best friend that he ever had.

"Is that Ashley?" he asked, turning away from the mess. Devil covered the head up.

Pussy had dealt with a lot of shit in his time, but a severed head from the body of a friend was not one of them. When he was around, the *enemy* died, not one of his friends or the men he trusted with his life. This was why he went on the road. Once he was there, no one could get to him to make him care.

"Yes." Devil stood as well, moving away from the desk.

"He killed her when he offered her protection." Pussy paced the length of the office. He was pissed. No, he was beyond pissed. He would like to kill the bastard with his own bare hands.

"Yes. We were meeting up with The Skulls for help, and now Tiny and his boys are in as much shit as we are. He's been assigned the run with us to collect the girls."

Pussy shook his head. "A man this powerful, commanding this many men has to be seen on the Feds' radar. There's no way they wouldn't be watching him."

"Then we've got more reason to watch our backs. Any Feds or undercover agents on this job are risking their lives to bring down as many people as possible. If not, then Gonzalez is just a criminal who's been able to stay under the alert. It takes time for people to catch on when girls go missing. Take one or two from a state, no one sees what is truly happening. Either way, I'm not going down for this fucker. We keep our head above water. No more undercover deals. The boys using drugs, get them into rehab. I don't want any of this crap to fall back on us. I've got enough to deal with without drawing more attention our way."

Pussy stared at the box thinking about Ashley. "Shit, who's going to tell Mia?"

Curse's woman had been best friends with Ashley. Their friendship had been strange. They were like chalk and cheese, yet they stuck by each other through everything. Even Pussy admired Mia for what she had done to protect Ashley when they were younger. Mia had killed Ashley's father when she'd stumbled onto him raping her.

"She's already been told. Curse is consoling her right now." Devil looked down at the floor. "We've got work to do."

After he followed his president out of the office, they called everyone around them. There was nothing Pussy or Devil could do or say to make this any easier.

Ashley was dead, Gonzalez had done it, and there was fuck all he could do about it.

Separating the drug users from the group, Pussy started to make arrangements to have them booked into a rehab center. Nothing made any sense to him. Fuck, he needed to get his dick in a tight cunt before he went insane.

****

Sasha leaned against the wall of the library. She listened to the hustle and bustle of everyone going past. None of them paid her any attention. She didn't mean anything to anyone. There was a time when people would stop and say hello. Then her mother had married her stepfather, and now no one wanted to say anything to her.

In one blow, the world had gone from a bright, shiny place to dark. The sudden blindness had been hard for the doctors to understand. She knew why, and so did her stepfather. It was the family secret that no one else could know the truth of. Before the world went dark she'd loved to read about everything. There was a time she'd wanted to be a doctor, but there was no chance of that happening anymore. She was blind, so there was no way for her to treat the sick without being able to look. He'd taken everything from her, and yet she was more dependent on him now than ever before.

In the medical book she'd read before she went blind she knew that an extreme blow to the head like in car accidents or falls down the stairs could cause amnesia or blindness, some sorts temporary and others not. She hadn't died this time, but her stepfather liked to cause pain if he was pushed too far.

God, she hated him. She hated relying on him as well. All of the friends she had in school were long gone. Everyone was afraid of her stepfather and wouldn't come near her. She was twenty years old, and no one gave a shit about her. Her own mother was doped up on prescription medication while she suffered. She still loved her mother, but the woman was emotionally blind to the truth of her stepfather's cruelty.

Fortunately, the bastard only liked to hurt. He wasn't interested in getting his rocks off, as otherwise she would have been in trouble. Her stepfather still liked her mother for what he wanted in the bedroom. It was strange the control he liked to exhibit over Sasha.

She tensed as someone leaned against the wall next to her.

"Who's there?" she asked.

"Don't worry, baby. I'm not going to hurt you."

Sasha frowned. "Shane?"

"Yeah, you remember my voice?"

Remember? His voice was the only thing she could think about. The way her body awakened at the simple tones of his voice surprised her. The guys in high school had never been successful in making her feel anything. She'd never been great with understanding what boys or men wanted from her.

She nodded her head, staring straight ahead of her. Was the parking lot completely tarmacked over, or were there flower beds dotted around to give it a more caring feel? Why was she thinking about the parking lot when Shane was close to her?

"You shouldn't be out on your own."

"I'm waiting for my stepdad to pick me up."

"And he left you on your own?"

Not down to choice.

There were still some men, rich men, her stepfather had to suck up to. She didn't know the man's name even though he had a rich Italian accent. Anyway, rich Italian accent guy had advised for her to go to the library. She got away with the help of a kind sounding secretary. Sasha hadn't recognized the smell or sound of the woman helping her.

"I guess."

"Look, I know you can't see me and I'm sorry about that, but I just needed to see you."

She frowned. "You sound sad."

"Shit, you're blind. You're not supposed to know that kind of stuff."

"You can't disguise your voice." She folded her arms for something to do.

What did he look like? She imagined lots of tattoos and a hard body like some of the action stars she used to watch.

"I just lost someone who meant the world to me," he said.

"I'm so sorry."

"She was a beautiful woman."

Jealousy struck her hard. He loved another woman. But then guilt hit at her thoughts. He didn't deserve her to be angry. They hadn't agreed to anything, and this was the first time he'd actually talked to her.

Had he sought her out?

No, that was crazy. There was no way Shane would seek her out. She would bet every cent she owned that he was never without female company.

"Was she your wife or girlfriend?"

Shane laughed. "No, she wasn't my girlfriend. She was a club whore. Don't worry, pet. You don't have a clue what's going on. I just needed to talk to someone, and I don't know why the fuck I thought to come to you."

She heard him move, and she reached out, holding onto thin air. Growling in frustration she took a step forward and tripped. Sasha let out a little squeal just before he caught her. His arms banded around her body, holding her steady.

"What the fuck, baby?"

Her head pressed against his chest as he spoke. The vibrations were amazing to feel. His body had to be twice the size of hers. The moment he touched her, those large hands wrapped around her body, she felt safe. This was insane. She couldn't be feeling this way about a man she didn't even know.

"I'm sorry. I just didn't want you to go." She steadied herself.

Shane walked her back until the wall stopped her from going anywhere.

"Shane, what's going on?" she asked. Heat bloomed inside her body. She wanted him to kiss her lips.

Shit, her fantasies were so fucking childish. She had nothing to compare them to.

"I don't go by Shane, baby. I go by Pussy."

She frowned. "What?"

"It's my club name. I like to eat pussy and drown in pussy. It's my name, and it's time you recognized it."

His breath fanned her face. Licking her lips, she wished she could stare into his eyes.

"You are so beautiful."

Tension built inside her, and she jerked as his lips brushed across hers.

"It's okay, baby. I won't hurt you. Don't listen to the shit people say. We don't believe in hurting people."

Pussy's lips crashed over hers. She ran her hands up his chest to circle his neck as one hand gripped her ass tightly.

He pulled her close, and she felt the heat of his body through the thin dress she wore. The hard ridge of his cock pressed to her body. He was long and thick. She could make out the feel of him even through their clothing.

As suddenly as he was there, kissing her, he was gone.

"Shit, I shouldn't have done that. Forget this ever happened."

In the next moment he was gone, leaving her lips tingling all over.

Chapter One

One month later

The Skulls were now part of Gonzalez's delivery boys just like the Chaos Bleeds crew. They'd collected the girls from one of the containers near the bay several miles away and distributed them to where Gonzalez wanted them working. Some of the girls were working in the strip club. Vincent was not in the best of moods to be handing out sex. Pussy hated the new life. There was no laughter, no freedom, and they were all waiting for the shit to hit the fan.

For the first time ever, between the two clubs there was no hope. The last visit to Fort Wills Pussy had felt the change inside everyone. Butch had to work to earn back the title of being a member, and shit was going on there that Pussy didn't understand. Tiny hadn't just accepted Butch back into the fold like everyone thought would happen. He was waiting for the right time when Lash returned to have a vote.

Nothing was worth what they were all going through. A lot of the men were in rehab to combat their drug addictions. Pussy was pleased he'd not succumbed to any addiction other than a nice warm cunt. He'd visited a couple of the men while they were coming out of it. The sight wasn't pretty.

Pushing all the nastiness away, Pussy stared at the woman bent over in front of him. Her creamy cunt was on display waiting for his cock, but he wasn't feeling it. He'd been fucking her moments ago, but now he couldn't forget the sight of his brothers barfing up and shaking as the drugs were slowly releasing from their systems.

"Are you okay?" the woman asked, glancing over

her shoulder to look at him. He wasn't interested in looking the woman in the face. She wasn't Ashley, and she wasn't Sasha either. The woman in front of him was just a willing cunt for him to lose some time outside of his head. Life was crap at the clubhouse. Everywhere they went, life was shit, and Devil was being more cautious than he'd ever been in his life.

"Yeah, baby. I'm good." He collapsed to the bed. Even though his cock was rock hard, he wasn't in the mood to do any of the work.

"Do you want me to take care of you?" The woman was naked with a set of fake tits and ass to go with it. He smiled up at her.

"Sure, babe. Work those lips on my dick." Placing a hand behind his head, he stared up at the ceiling as she cooed and pretended to purr like a kitten. Rolling his eyes, he let out a sigh. There was a time when a woman wouldn't get any sleep once he got his hands on them. Now, he was fucking useless. No one was going to want to fuck him at this rate.

She grasped his cock, removed the condom, and started to lick the tip. Glancing down, he watched her lapping up his pre-cum as if it was a delicacy she'd never tasted before.

"Yeah, baby, take it all in." He didn't know her name, and he didn't care either.

Thrusting his hips into her waiting mouth, he closed his eyes, picturing Sasha with her lips around his cock. The little bitch had been invading his thoughts more and more regularly. No matter what he did, she wouldn't leave him alone. The few conversations they'd had were not ground breaking, but he played them over and over in his mind. The kiss they'd shared had been fleeting and tame, yet it got him hot every time he thought about it. When it came to Sasha, all of his thoughts turned him on.

He thought about her lips wrapped around his cock. Her long brown hair cascading over his body as she sucked him off was too much of a fantasy for him to ignore. Gripping the woman's head, he slammed in deep, forcing her to take more of him.

Within seconds he released into her mouth and wouldn't let her go until she swallowed every single drop of his cum. When it was over he ordered her out of his room. The woman had the grace not argue or throw shit at him and left. The sweet-butts knew they were all in trouble and didn't argue when an order came their way. Everyone did as Devil ordered the first time without making any waves.

Lying back on his bed, Pussy stared up at the ceiling. Someone knocked on his door, and he ignored the sound.

Seconds later, Death came into view.

"You ignoring everyone now?" Death asked, taking a seat on the bed.

"No. I'm choosing to ignore every fucker that tries to get into my room. I'm not called Pussy for nothing. The women will all be fighting if I start answering shit." He flipped onto his side and leaned over the bed to grab a cigarette. Lighting the tip, he lay back down, inhaling the nicotine into his lungs.

"The women are no longer leaving your room looking satisfied, Pussy. Maybe you're losing your touch." Death sparked up a cigarette and sat on the floor with his back leaning against the bed.

"Nah, the women are just not used to me only taking care of myself. I'm not interested in making friends with the bitches. They want to suck and fuck cock, then they can. I just don't always return the favor." He blew out a ring of smoke thinking about the brown-haired beauty he'd kissed a month ago.

"That doesn't sound like you. Does this have to do with Ashley?" Death asked.

Thinking about Ashley made him sad, but it didn't stop him from fucking other women. Now, thinking about Sasha stopped him from wanting to be with other women. It pissed him off. One simple kiss shouldn't have left him feeling this way. Rubbing at his chest, he wondered what the hell was happening to him.

"No, it doesn't."

"Curse hasn't been able to bring Mia to the club. She's sobbing all the time, and he can't get her to eat. He's really struggling with this shit." Death blew out a ring.

"What the fuck do you want me to do?" Pussy asked.

"Nothing. I'm telling you, you're not the only one missing Ashley. I'm not an idiot, Pussy. Don't treat me like one. You and Ashley were close. I know you were never going to give her a ring or promise her forever, but you would never turn your back on her either."

He thought about what Death said. "We got her killed."

"Yes, we all did. The club got her killed. We should have stopped her from going with Gonzalez. There's a lot of shit we should have done, but we didn't, and now we're the ones paying the price." Death let out a sigh. "Shit is getting nasty, Pussy. You need to start playing the game."

"Life is not a game."

"Fuck, Pussy. Stop being an ass. Ashley's dead and gone. You're going to sit around and die because she's not going to be coming around anymore. Gonzalez fucked with us. It's time for us to fuck back." Death stubbed out his cigarette and walked off.

Lying back on the bed, Pussy thought about what he said. He'd not gone to see Mia ever since he saw Ashley's severed head. Climbing off the bed, he took a quick shower and headed toward the spare ranch style house on the outskirts of Piston County. After parking up his bike, he knocked on the door and waited for Curse to let him inside.

Curse opened up the door looking like the weight of the world was on his shoulders.

"Hey, man, does Devil want me?" he asked.

"Nah, I've come to see you both." In the background he heard Mia crying. "She not taking it well?"

Curse looked behind him, shaking his head. "No, she's not taking any shit well. She doesn't want to have a burial until we've got the whole body. I've told it would never happen. Gonzalez wouldn't give it to us, but she won't budge. The girls were closer than sisters. This bond, it's killing her. I stopped her from seeing the head, but shit, this is killing her."

Swallowing past the lump in his throat, Pussy stared at the ground. "I should have come to see her the moment I knew."

"Pussy, don't do this. I'm sorry I've not been there for you. My woman comes first unless I'm needed for club business."

"I'm here to speak with Mia."

Curse's shoulders slumped. "I don't think that's a good idea."

"Let him in, Curse. He's got a right to be here."

Looking over his friend's shoulder, he saw Mia. She looked a mess. Her raven hair showed she hadn't even bothered to brush the long locks. Her pale face looked drawn, and he saw the signs of the weight loss she'd suffered through lack of eating in the last month.

"Come in," Curse said.

Brushing past his friend Pussy went straight to Mia and tugged her in his arms for a hug. She sobbed. Her body shook as he held her tightly. "I'm so sorry. I miss her so much," he said.

Tears filled his eyes as he thought about Ashley's charming smile. Her life had ended way too suddenly.

"I know, Pussy. She wouldn't want you to be feeling sorry. You didn't do this."

"I shouldn't have let her go."

"None of us should. We can't blame each other." Pussy couldn't stop the guilt. He knew deep down there was nothing he or the club could have done. Ashley had been determined to go, and in turn, it had gotten her killed.

Pussy knew where the blame was. Staring past her shoulder, he watched Curse walk into the kitchen. Any other time Curse would have kicked his ass for touching his woman. This was not sexual, and both of them were mourning a woman they'd both lost.

Mia released him, walking into the sitting room. "I know I look a mess."

Running fingers through his hair, Pussy took a seat.

"Please, forgive me," he said.

"What? Why?"

"I should have fought for her."

"Ashley wasn't your old lady. She was always so stubborn and thought she could do whatever she liked without getting hurt." Tears fell from Mia's eyes. "Someone finally caught her."

He wasn't leaving until he helped out his brother. Curse deserved to have his woman back, and if Pussy could help, he'd be more than happy about it.

****

Sasha let out a sigh as she listened to her mother apologize for embarrassing her stepfather. Kenneth Carmichael was a monster of the worst kind. He made others around him feel small and incompetent. Sasha hated him and would love to see the smile get wiped off his face.

You'll never see any smile getting wiped off any face.

She started to frown. Reaching out, she felt along the wall counting the steps until she had to turn a corner. Her life was confined to the house and wherever Kenneth wanted to leave her. He controlled every element of her life.

Get out.

Taking three more steps, she leaned down feeling the bed. Running her hand across the bed, she took a seat and let out a sigh. She recalled the trauma she'd suffered at Kenneth hands. Sasha had been arguing with Kenneth over her privacy being invaded. He had just stormed into her room as if he had a right to be there. Their fighting had turned aggressive. She recalled him slapping her, and he slammed her against the wall, then thrown her down the stairs.

She'd banged her head on the way down, breaking her arm and leg in the process. When she woke up in the hospital she'd not been able to see. That was over four years ago. Waking up and not being able to see she had expected something to be done to Kenneth after the attack. By the time he showed up in her room, she knew something had happened.

With her being passed out, unconscious, he'd fed them a story of how she'd been fighting with him before she stumbled and fell downstairs. Not once did he tell the truth, and worse, her mother believed him. She didn't fight for her or even question Sasha's side of things.

Instead, because of her mother's love for Kenneth, they were still living with the man who blinded her. Kenneth was a respected member of Piston County, handsome, and a smooth talker. He got away with it. No one would hear anything bad said about him even if it was the truth. She was trapped with no way of getting out. Not only would no one believe her, but she couldn't walk out of the house. Her life was totally dependent on him. Twenty years old and she was dependent on a man she despised. Her mother begged her for trust, and because she loved her mother, she gave him a chance. Her mother didn't know the truth of what happened. Now, there was no way of Sasha's ever getting out.

She thought about Pussy, Shane, whatever his name was. She pressed a hand to her lips. The kiss had awoken something inside her. Her nights were filled with hot sexual dreams. She couldn't see what he was doing, but she certainly could feel it.

Her mother knocked on the door before entering. Kenneth would have just barged into the room with no consideration for her privacy. She knew her stepfather hated her.

"Hey, honey. I've brought you some food."

Counting the steps, she heard how unsteady her mother was on her feet. She must have hit the gin hard this time. In answer to the verbal abuse Kenneth threw at her, her mother had turned to drink and prescription drugs. Even with the addictions, her mother was a beautiful woman, a stunner. What a fun way for them to live.

The tray of food was placed on the counter that her mother then pushed in front of her.

"Lift your hands up, honey."

She did as her mother asked. Seconds later her mother touched her with shaking hands as she brought her palms down either side of the tray.

"Here is your fork and knife."

Closing her eyes, Sasha gritted her teeth at how useless her situation was.

This is your life.

The doctors, in the beginning, were not sure if the blindness was permanent or not. Four years down the line, Sasha had long given up hope of her sight returning, and the doctors had also said that the damage was by now irreversible.

"Now, I don't want you to worry about your father's and my little spat."

"He's not my father." No, her father had died in the Marines when she was ten, leaving behind a wife and daughter. Kenneth had come into their lives by the time she was eleven with his fake promises and fake lives.

"Don't say stuff like that. He's been wonderful to us."

"You're an addict, Mom, and I'm blind. He's torn us apart."

She heard her mother sob. In the past whenever her mother was hurt, she'd press a hand to her lips, gasping. Feeling like a total bitch, she apologized. Her mother was completely oblivious to the problems Kenneth caused. If Sasha didn't love her mother and remember all the times they were together with fondness, she's have been long gone by now. The drink and drugs had turned the woman she knew into something unrecognizable.

"I'm sorry, Mom. I hate having to go through this." She reached up to touch her face.

"Oh, honey. It's no trouble. I love being able to take care of you when other mothers are fretting about what their kids are getting up to."

The bed dipped, and Sasha's senses were flooded

by the extreme scent of perfume, another of Kenneth's demands from her mother.

"Why was he shouting?" she asked, trying to distract her mother.

"I was stupid and put too much pepper in the mashed potatoes. It was a simple mistake. I messed up."

Seriously, Mom, over-peppered mashed potatoes. Don't you see what's wrong with that? Please, see how bad he is and realize it's only going to get worse.

Sasha had no choice in her situation. The people believed she was clumsy and had fallen down the stairs, banging her head. Her mother, however, could change all that if only she had the courage to do so.

"Try them. Please let me know what you think."

Her mother was an amazing cook. Before Kenneth turned up, Sasha would sit in the kitchen for hours at a time trying food she concocted. Her mother had a knack in the kitchen, and it was where her mother got the most comfort. The only food she was allowed to cook now was of the gourmet kind, and Sasha hated it.

Tasting the potatoes, she tried not to wince at the blandness of them. They were heavily peppered and salted.

"They're nice, Mom."

"You're an awful liar."

Chuckling, Sasha ate her food relishing every second her mother sat with her. Most of the time, her mother was trying to please Kenneth and staying far away from her, only spending rare moments with her. When she got chance to talk with her mother, she did try to get her to go to the cops or someone who'd listen. After four years, Sasha still hadn't given up hope that the mother she used to know was still in there.

Sasha was twenty years old and yet felt more like a child than ever before.

There was so much she couldn't do. Whenever she started to get confident with moving around, Kenneth would order the maid to make changes, causing her to bang into stuff.

"Mom, what do you know about the Chaos Bleeds crew? You know, the biker group in town."

Her mother tensed at her side. She was sitting close enough for Sasha to feel the sudden change within her. Eating some of her food, Sasha took each bite carefully so as not to make a mess of herself. She'd learned early not to be greedy or she'd be wearing her food rather than enjoying it.

"They're ruffians, all of them. Don't let your father hear you talk about them."

He's not my father.

"I won't. I just overheard some people in the library giggling about them. I just wondered who they were. I've never seen them before."

She wasn't lying. The rumors were rife about the biker group in town. She'd been reading Braille while women had been giggling over the men who were part of the club. A couple of times she'd heard Pussy's name mentioned, and now that she knew it was Shane, she found herself listening more and more.

"You really shouldn't concern yourself with them, honey, for your own sake. They're a curse to the world and one I hope to see gone from our lovely town."

The next moment her mother stopped talking, and the silence unnerved Sasha. Seconds later, she heard the reason why.

"What's going on in here?" Kenneth asked.

"I'm just talking with Sasha while she eats."

"You served her those shit mashed potatoes? Really? I thought you said you could cook." The way his voice dropped Sasha knew he was sneering, and it angered her more than anything.

"I like them," Sasha said.

"Yeah, only because you're not seeing the shit you're eating. Take the food away, now. Go and have a fucking drink. It's all you're good for." The fork was tugged out of her grip. Her mother's hand shook. Sasha felt it from the small contact she had with her. She wanted to reach out and shake her mother, to wake her up to the monster he was. The door to her room was closed. She wasn't an idiot. Kenneth was still in the room waiting to have his say.

"What?" she asked, resting her hands in her lap to try to calm her nerves. Since the first attack, Kenneth only ever hurt by gripping her too tightly or giving her a slap from time to time. He'd not lashed out as much. She figured it was down to fear as he'd given off the persona of being the concerned stepfather. Anything happened to her now and things would look suspicious.

"Be careful how you talk to me, girl."

She tensed up, sinking her nails into her skin.

"We've got to go out tomorrow. I'll be dropping you off at the library."

"I could stay home."

"I don't want you to stay home. We need to be seen. After tonight your mother will be useless. She'll be swigging from the bottle as we speak."

Closing her eyes, she tried to shut out his words. She hated him. The anger at what he'd done to her mother was still raw. He'd turned her into some kind of suburban housewife for him to toy with whenever he felt like it. Sasha despised him and hoped he died a long, slow death.

"You'll do tomorrow. The town will see how well you're doing, and then I can get to my meeting."

"Who are you meeting?" she asked.

"None of your business. Play your part, and I won't let anything bad happen to your mother or you."

Pausing, Sasha turned her head in the direction of his voice, opening her eyes even though she couldn't see.

"What?"

"You heard me. I've got ways of making people disappear. Think about that the next time one of the Chaos Bleeds scum comes near you."

The door to her room closed behind her. Who the fuck was Kenneth Carmichael, and how could he get rid of her mother? She didn't have the time to think about it. For now she'd do exactly as he said without causing any waves. Sasha wouldn't let anything happen to her mother, if she could help it.

Chapter Two

The night spent with Mia and Curse hadn't been a total waste. Pussy rode behind them as they all headed toward the clubhouse. Mia had taken a bath, brushed her hair, and changed her clothes. She'd not smelled that bad, but it hadn't been pretty, or at least it hadn't been to him.

Pulling into the clubhouse parking lot, he saw Devil picking up his daughter and son as Lexie walked alongside him into the main house.

"What's going on?" Pussy asked, climbing off his bike. He never wore a helmet if he could help it. The point of being on the road was to feel the wind in his hair, across his face. The helmet would stop that. Pussy would do a lot of things for the club, but wearing a helmet wasn't one of them.

"Nothing. I'd feel happier if my family was close by me." Devil shook his head as he walked into the clubhouse. The whole story would come out soon.

"Devil, baby, you don't need to worry," Lexie said, taking her daughter out of Devil's arms.

"I'm not worrying, but I'm not having you in harm's way, either. You and the kids mean too fucking much to me. Speaking of kids, I've ordered Judi and Ripper home as well. They're packing their shit up. Vincent and Phoebe will be back at the clubhouse soon as well." Devil didn't lose his stride, talking as he escorted his family inside. Pussy kept up with them wondering what the hell had happened.

"That will make it a full house, Devil. You can't expect the men to put up with the kids."

"Tiny does it with his club. They can't hack this life, then they're out. It's as simple as that."

They all went silent, entering the clubhouse

29

together. Devil stopped and covered his son's eyes then started cursing. Glancing around, Pussy saw the problem. First, for him, was the mess, and then he caught sight of the naked women and club members, along with all the alcohol on display.

"Fuckers, get your shit out of the main hall. Until further notice, sex is done in the confines of your own fucking room. You don't have a room, then get out. I'm not in the mood to be ordering this shit around." Devil shoved one naked man off the table.

Pussy didn't recognize him, so he must have been a hanger on.

"Devil, this is the clubhouse. They can be here like this," Lexie said.

"I've got to make a call to Tiny." Devil turned, looking at Pussy. "Take my woman and kids and get them settled. I don't want to worry about her safety for the next five minutes."

Taking Edward from Devil's arms, Pussy nodded. "On it, boss."

His president walked toward his office. Turning to Lexie, Pussy saw the concern on her face.

"Come on. I better do what he says otherwise it's going to get worse for me." He took her hand, leading her away from the chaos in the main room.

"It's all going to get a lot worse, right?" Lexie asked.

"I don't know." He walked up the long flight of stairs, going to the top floor of the clubhouse. The top floor was Devil's and Lexie's room. "Are you going to tell me what happened, or do I have to guess?"

Lexie sighed, moving her daughter to her other hip.

"I got a visit from Frederick yesterday."

Pussy paused, turning to look at her. "What?"

"Can we get to the room? She's heavy, and I'll tell you what you want to know."

He didn't respond but picked up the pace to get her to the main room. Did he want to know what Frederick was doing back in Piston County? Crap, if he was back and they'd not had a visit then it could only mean that he was here to see someone else. He didn't like it. Pussy didn't like the threat this man posed to all of them.

Inside the room he saw the windows were all closed. Putting Edward down in a safe place, Pussy went around the room, opening the windows to let some fresh air into the room.

Lexie sighed as a breeze rushed through the room.

"I hate this. I hate how paranoid he's becoming," Lexie said.

Turning to face her, Pussy saw Lexie was pale. She looked ill.

"What's going on?"

"Devil was at the clubhouse yesterday, and I didn't give it a thought to check who was calling. Phoebe calls around, and Judi still uses the doorbell to visit. She's walked in too many times on me and Devil going at it."

Pussy chuckled. Judi saw Lexie and Devil as her parents. Seeing your parents having sex would upset anyone.

"Anyway, I didn't check, and Frederick was at the door. He wanted to be let in. After everything that happened, I didn't want to anger him."

"You let him in. Do you know about Ashley?"

"I know everything that goes on at this club, Pussy. Devil doesn't keep secrets from me, even though I imagine he'd like to try it. I wouldn't let him. Chaos

Bleeds is my family as much as it's his." Lexie shrugged. The shirt she wore fell off her shoulder.

"Did he hurt you?"

"No, Frederick didn't hurt me. He asked to have tea and cake with me. The kids were playing, and I didn't want to piss him off. He talked about loyalty and how important loyalty was." She ran a hand over her face. "I don't know what he's trying to do, but I think he's going to try and break The Skulls and Chaos Bleeds apart."

Pussy frowned. "What?"

"He implied that someone within Tiny's club has lost all their loyalty. I don't know what to make of it. Devil arrived and freaked out. He didn't start shooting Frederick's ass, but he was close." Lexie blew out a breath. "I wish we could go back, you know? Go back to when shit was simple and I was pissed at Devil for stupid shit."

He knew what she meant. "Devil's always going to be like this around you. He loves you, Lex. You can't let this upset you. Also, you know he's going to protective of you. You're his woman, the mother of his children. Even after everything you've been through, you're fucking hot."

She started laughing. "Thank you, Pussy. You're the best." She moved closer to him and kissed his cheek. "Go on. Go and enjoy your freedom while Devil allows it. He's going to call for us all to be on lockdown. We'll all suffer then."

Nodding, he made sure she was okay before heading out. Dropping down into Death's room, he watched his friend riding a bitch's ass. Whistling, he caught Death's attention. He told him everything that Lexie had told him.

"No shit. What's the fucker up to?" Death asked. He stayed still inside the whore's body.

"I don't know. I've got a feeling he's trying to put a wedge between us and The Skulls."

"Good way to go about it. Make us afraid to trust Tiny and his crew." Death shook his head. "Where are you going?"

"I'm heading out. If we're going on lockdown, I'm getting some road time in. I need to clear my head before it's trapped in the same place."

Closing the door, he left Death to the whore he was fucking. Pulling out his keys, he headed down to the main part of the clubhouse as Devil was coming upstairs.

"What's Tiny got to say about it?" Pussy asked.

"He says it's all lies."

"And you don't believe him?" Leaning against the wall, Pussy noticed how tired his president looked. Settling down was supposed to have been fun. This was more stress than being on the road all the time.

"I don't know what to believe. Frederick is a complete bastard, but he warned me that not all is well in Tiny's crew. Either way, I don't trust Frederick. He clearly has an end game, and I want no part in it. The last thing we need right now is to start causing problems with Tiny. I happen to like the bastard."

"We've dealt with members turning on each other. It's what you and Tiny did with The Darkness."

"The Darkness didn't deserve loyalty. They were a bunch of fucking rapists. That situation is different from now. Tiny wouldn't risk his club or his woman's life. Stop worrying about what Frederick said. He was supposed to take care of Ashley, yet he killed her. Shit, I've got too much shit to lose. I've got to go and think." Devil pushed past him.

"You know, this could just be shit to make us weak. We fight Tiny, they fight us, and we cull each other. Then Frederick sweeps in and takes out the rest of us. Have you thought about that?"

"I've thought of everything, Pussy. I don't know what to think anymore." Devil stopped talking and made his way upstairs.

Conversation was terminated.

Blowing out a breath, Pussy ignored the bitches cleaning and went back to the parking lot. Straddling his bike, he turned on the engine and pulled out of the compound. He needed a clear head to help his president, as otherwise he'd be no good.

Being part of Chaos Bleeds came with a price. Pussy knew that the moment he signed up to the club over ten years ago. He had been twenty-three years old, and he'd won a fight in a bar when Devil offered him a place in the club. To earn extra cash, Pussy had fought in any underground fighting competition he could. Even back then, his reputation of loving pussy preceded him. His fighting name was Pussy, making a lot of fighters think he wasn't great in the ring. He soon shut them up once he started hitting and didn't stop.

Pussy was out on the open road for over an hour before the hunger hit him and he realized he'd not eaten a thing for breakfast. Turning back, he headed toward the diner for some food. The ride hadn't cleared his head enough, but some food might help.

****

Kenneth had left her alone in the diner. Sasha wanted to go to the library, but instead he'd left her in the diner, and she was too scared to make it over the road to the library. The women who served her food and drink didn't give her more time than was necessary. The noise kept her rooted to the spot. She pulled out her music player, placed the headphones in, and turned her music on. Moving slowly, she reached out to take the cup of hot chocolate and brought it to her lips. The liquid was warm.

She kept her sunglasses on inside the diner. Being on her own, she didn't want to be caught staring when she couldn't see anything.

Tapping her finger on the table, she bounced her head in time to the music. What was the point in bringing her out of the house if he was only going to leave her like this?

Sasha knew why. It was just another side to his cruelty. This was why she could never be alone again. The fear of what the outside world would do to her scared the shit out of her. All the plans she'd made with her father growing up crashed around her. They used to talk about going travelling around Europe, seeing the Northern Lights, or visiting the Grand Canyon. None of that was going to happen to her. She was doomed to spend the rest of her life in Piston County, never knowing what sex felt like, dying a virgin.

God, her thoughts were depressing. She hated her life.

She gasped as someone tapped her hand. Jerking the head phones off, she tried to hear who was talking.

"You've got a beautiful singing voice, Sasha."

"Pussy?"

"The one and only. Budge up." He sat down beside her. His large body nudged her up to the side of the booth. She didn't bother glancing around trying to look for Kenneth. What was the point?

"I was singing?" She couldn't have been singing.

"Yeah, babe, you were. Singing loud enough to catch my attention. You weren't too bad either."

He leaned over her, and she heard the paper rustling. Menu?

"I'm sorry. I didn't mean to distract you from your lunch."

"You didn't distract me. It was nice to hear something other than complaining customers." He flicked over the menu. "Everything here sounds like shit. I fancy some decent food. Do you want to come with me on my bike?" he asked.

Her heart pounded inside her chest.

Kenneth?

The hope died as instantly as it sparked. "No, I can't."

"Your stepfather's not here. He causes you shit, I'll deal with him. Do you want to go with me or not?"

Did she ever!

"Can I ride with you? I can't see."

"You can hold onto me, baby. I'll keep you safe. Do you want to live a little?"

She reached out, gripping his arm. "Please, take me with you."

He held her hand, and she climbed out of the booth. Pussy didn't let go of her hand, which she was thankful for. She didn't know if she'd make it outside without passing out or looking like an idiot. He took his time to lead her to the door. She counted the steps from the booth to the door. Outside, the sound of the busy town caught her unawares. She stumbled against Pussy's back. He banded an arm around her waist.

"Don't you worry about a thing, baby. I've got you."

She liked being pressed against him. He held onto her, and together they walked down the street. Sasha imagined people staring at them, wondering what the hell she was doing with him. She didn't care what they all thought. In her mind, Pussy was a sexy man, a sinfully sexy man.

"Right, we're at my bike. I've got a helmet for you to wear. I'm going to place it over your head. I'll be gentle, okay?"

"Yes."

Standing perfectly still, she waited for him to place the helmet over her head. He secured the buckle underneath her chin.

"There, it's pretty solid." He took hold of her hand. "Keep your hand on my shoulder. You've got to trust me, and you'll get on my bike without a hitch, okay?"

"Okay." Gripping his shoulder, she couldn't help but notice how thick his shoulders were. The guy was huge. He moved forward, and she went on her toes to keep hold of him.

"Now, cock your leg over. When you feel your cunt on the seat, settle in," he said.

"What?"

Had she heard him correctly? Heat went straight between her thighs at his words. No, surely she'd been imagining things. There was no way he would say stuff like that.

"You heard me. Don't expect nice words from me. I call it like I see it. I can promise you, you'll be safe with me. I'm not interested in hurting women."

Unlike Kenneth, her stepfather. Did he know about Kenneth or even suspect the other man of being a total bastard?

Flinging her leg over the side of the bike, she settled into the seat, feeling happy to have achieved something without looking stupid.

"Hold onto me tightly."

Wrapping her arms around his waist, she held on as tightly as she could. "Is this okay?" she asked.

"Yeah, baby. It's all fine to me."

The engine purred to life. Resting her face against his back, excitement filled every part of her core.

Smiling, she let out a squeal as he pulled away from where he was parked. She kept her eyes closed, holding on tightly to Pussy as he drove the bike. Sasha didn't have a clue who he was or even if she could trust him, but she did.

He hadn't hurt her yet.

He's not going to hurt you.

She didn't get the vibe from him that she did from Kenneth. If he wanted to hurt her, he could have already. Instead, he'd made her feel more independent and kissed her in the few times they'd been together. She was losing her mind when it came to this man. Keeping her arms around him, she was aware of how hard and muscular he was.

Sasha didn't have a clue where they were going, and she didn't care.

Time passed, and for the first time since her blindness, Sasha felt free, happy.

The sun beat down on them. Kenneth would lose his mind when he found her gone.

This is your chance to go.

Pushing all thoughts aside she simply basked in the time of not being controlled by a man she despised.

The bike soon came to a stop, and she was overcome by the most amazing smells.

"Now, this is a steakhouse," Pussy said. His voice vibrated his body. She loved the sound of his voice. Her own pussy grew warm at the feel of him between her thighs.

She was a virgin, and there hadn't been any way for her to change that status in her life. Fear suddenly gripped her at the thought of what Kenneth would do. She hadn't pushed him to attack her again, but she'd been too dependent on him to push him away. At night she heard him with her mother and knew he still desired her. Did he want her out of the way so her mother was no longer dealing with her? Ever since her blindness, her mother spent more time with her, not enough time for it to matter to Sasha, but Kenneth always sounded angry whenever he found her mother in her room.

"Are you ready for some food?" he asked.

"I think you should take me back." She still kept her hands around his waist, not wanting to let him go.

"Why?"

"Kenneth, my stepdad, he's not going to like me being elsewhere." She shivered at the thought of his anger. Her mother didn't deserve this.

What about me? Do I deserve this?

Her life was at the mercy of the man who'd caused her blindness. She was trapped in a vicious cycle that Kenneth had created.

"Has he hurt you?" Pussy asked.

Biting her lip, she felt him move and loosened her hold on him.

"It's nothing."

Pussy helped her off the bike and removed the helmet she wore. His touch was sweet as he tilted her head back. "Don't lie to me."

She wished she could see his face. "What do you look like?" she asked.

Her cheeks heated at the questions. She tried to push out of his touch. He wouldn't release her.

"I swear to you, Sasha, I'm not going to hurt you."

Sasha had no reason to believe him, and yet she did.

"Yes, he's hurt me." The moment she released the words a great weight had been lifted off her shoulders. Collapsing against him, she started to cry, real large tears. His large arms banded around her.

"It's okay. I've got you, Sasha. I won't let that fucker hurt you again."

There was nothing he could do, but knowing that he cared meant a lot to her.

Closing her eyes, she let him hold her. What would it matter if he held her close? His hand ran down her back, resting at the base.

"How old are you?" he asked.

"I'm twenty."

"What are you still doing with the fucker who hurt you?" The anger in his voice made her tense.

"I don't have a choice. I can't live on my own."

"Your blindness shouldn't hold you back." He rubbed her cheek.

"I haven't always been blind."

"What? How the fuck is that possible?"

She dropped her head down. This was a mistake. She shouldn't have come.

"Fuck. You know what? Let's go and eat, and you can tell me your story. We're not leaving here until I get it."

****

Frederick Gonzalez stared at Kenneth Carmichael. The fucker was all about the money. He didn't care about Piston County or the life of his family; all he wanted was money. Devil didn't have a clue that Frederick had more than one person working for him. Kenneth gave him what he needed, an inside look into the running of the town. He'd been able to put one of his men on the town council who made decisions. In one of the old warehouses, he'd bought the property for half the cost and was now using it as a coke making plant.

Gonzalez was all about the business and the money. Small towns were the best place to start his organization. Cops were bought as they all needed the extra cash because there was no work. Fort Wills were falling in line, and he'd placed his men in the force. Whenever Tiny didn't do as he was told, his men would go into the clubhouse and make them hurt. The last raid that Frederick ordered to happen had taken their kids off them. The Skulls were all about the family, and it was because of that family that Frederick got his own way.

"One of the apartment blocks is the perfect place for you to set up girls. Pay the cops off and they can get the money you need for the girls," Kenneth said.

"When all this is over, what are you going to do?" Frederick asked, curious about the man he was doing business with.

Mingling with his staff and being part of the running of the business was why he was so successful. His own father had gotten lazy with the running of the business and things had started to slide. Nothing was going to slide while Frederick remained a threat.

"My wife, Penny, has a daughter. She's blind and a pain in the ass, but nothing can happen to her. When I'm ready to leave, the daughter is going to meet with a fucking accident. She's been a thorn in my side for too fucking long. I want her out of the way, but I don't want my wife to know. She still fucking loves her. When it's all over I'll make sure she gets off the bottle and pills and stays completely dependent on me. She'll do to amuse me for a nice long retirement. With Sasha out of the picture, her mother will depend on me for comfort, and I intend to be there when she needs me," Kenneth said, counting the notes as he stacked them in his briefcase.

Kenneth hadn't come from money, and he wasn't even part of the elite in Piston County. He was a criminal who'd learned how to defraud people, and that business had grown to being the messenger for Gonzalez.

Frederick was happy to help a man with a

business mind.

"So your wife doesn't have a clue about any of your plans to relocate after her daughter's death?"

"She doesn't know. Sasha's the kind of girl everyone likes. The only way to get rid of her is to make it look like an accident. I don't want anyone pointing the finger at me. In time, Penny will see we don't need kids to be happy. She'll see how perfect we are together. I'll keep her in her place." Kenneth rubbed his hands together.

Tapping his leg, Frederick wondered what his next move should be with Chaos Bleeds. The two MC clubs were like his new toys. He told them to jump, and they had no choice but to say how high. Frederick wondered how much he could push before they all started to crack.

Chapter Three

Finding a booth in the back, Pussy kept hold of Sasha's hand to make sure she didn't trip or fall. He needed to stem his anger, as otherwise he was going to lose it. From the first moment he saw Kenneth, he'd hated the bastard, and now, knowing he'd hurt Sasha, he wanted to hurt him. No man should scare a woman, especially his stepdaughter.

Seating her inside the booth, he slid opposite her. She kept her palms down on the table, and he noticed she bit her lip. Her eyes were wide as she glanced around. The noise in the steakhouse was small, but she looked nervous.

Reaching out, he placed his palm over her hand. "There's no need to be nervous. I'm here, and I won't leave you, not even to take a piss."

The waitress walked to the table.

"Hello, can I take your order?" The waitress popped gum. Her stomach was swollen, and she was clearly pregnant as she rubbed her stomach affectionately.

"I'll have a strong, black coffee. What do you want, babe?" he asked.

"Can I have a soda?" Sasha's voice was small.

"Sure thing. I'll be back after you've had time to peruse the menu." The woman wrote their orders down then left.

"Do you want me to read the menu to you?" he offered, gripping the menu in one hand as he held her other hand.

"You'd do that for me?"

"How else would you know what to eat if I didn't?" he asked, frowning.

"Kenneth doesn't give me chance to order my

own food. I eat what he orders."

Gritting his teeth, Pussy gazed down at the menu. His fist was about to get an appointment in Kenneth's fucking face. The more he heard about the uptight bastard, the more he hated him.

"I'm sorry. I really shouldn't be telling you this."

"Who should you be telling instead of me?" he asked, staring at her face. Fuck, she was so beautiful. Her skin was pale, and her dark brown hair shone as the sun glided over the strands. The thick length looked silky. He wanted to wrap the length around his wrist and tug on it. Would she gasp or cry out? His cock hardened at the thought of her on her knees taking his cock. He'd pull on her hair as he rammed inside her, going as deep as he could.

"I don't have anyone to tell anything to."

"What happened to your friends? You can't tell me you weren't liked?"

"After the accident that caused this," she touched her face, "I was pulled out of school. I've been taught at home. The school didn't have any way of supporting a blind person. I've been taught by tutors."

Pussy frowned. Her stepfather was pulling her away from everyone she knew.

"What about your mother?" he asked.

Sasha laughed. The sound was harsh and brittle. "A couple of years ago I'd have said she was amazing. Now, she finds love at the bottom of the bottle and some pills. She's not the best person to talk to right now, and she loves Kenneth." She leaned her chin on her palm. Her gaze was on his chest. He didn't know what to say to her.

She was a nicely rounded woman, curvy in all the right places. From what he saw, he knew she had a nice, large set of tits that would fill his hands. Her hips were large, and she had a rounded stomach.

"Where's your father?"

He wanted to know everything about her.

"He died in action, in Afghanistan. Mom met Kenneth a year or so afterward, and then they married not long after that." She traced a pattern on the table with her other hand. "Why do you want to know about my family?"

"You've not got much family, but I wanted to see what was happening in your life."

Pussy paused as the waitress handed them their drinks. "We've not looked over the menu yet."

"No problem, honey, take your time. Hold your hand up or holler when you want serving." The waitress didn't stick around. Keeping his gaze on Sasha, Pussy wondered what she was thinking.

"Why do you want to know? I'm not that important."

"You're important to me," he said.

She let out a gasp.

"You've not always been blind?" he asked, directing the conversation elsewhere.

"No, I've not. How have you been since you lost your friend?"

Her question caught him by surprise. Thinking about Ashley upset him.

"She died, and there's no changing that." He rubbed his palms down his legs.

"Do you blame yourself?"

"Yes, I do." Pussy wasn't going to lie to her. He didn't want to. Was this what Ripper and Curse went through with their women? Devil seemed to change overnight with Lexie.

"Why?"

"She did something for the club and died for it.

45

Ashley didn't deserve to be killed, but when I get the bastard responsible, I'll kill him."

He watched her tense.

"Are you afraid of me?" he asked.

Sasha didn't answer him. He watched her frown, but seconds later she shook her head. "No, I'm not."

"No, are you insane? I just told you I'd kill a man for killing my friend, and you're not afraid."

She ran a hand across the table. "I don't get you. Do you want me to be afraid of you, or do you want me to trust you?"

Letting out a sigh, he rubbed a hand across his face. "I'm sorry. Thinking about Ashley makes me mad, and I don't know what I'm saying."

"It's okay. You've never hurt me."

"You don't know me," he said. Didn't this woman have any gut reaction to the dangers out there?

"Kenneth did know me, and yet I'm blind because of him."

Her words forced him to pause as he looked down at the menu.

"What? He hurt you."

"No one knows what he did. The doctors think I was arguing with him over something silly and I fell down the stairs. I was told trauma to the head can cause blindness. Kenneth hurt me, and since then I've been blind, depending on him to take care of me." She stopped talking. He saw her lip wobble. "My mom can't do anything. She's scared of him, I'm sure of it."

"He caused your blindness, and now you're having to rely on him. Who takes care of you?" he asked.

"No one. My mom and Kenneth take turns to get me out of the house. He rearranges the furniture so I can't remember the layout of the room." She stopped. "I really shouldn't be telling you this."

Pussy opened his mouth to talk to her when the sound of her stomach rumbling caught his attention. "You're hungry?"

"Yes, I've not had any breakfast."

Cursing his interest in her life, he started to read off the menu. None of the food registered in his mind as spoke the words out loud.

"Oh, I like the sound of the spicy cheeseburger. Could I have all of that with extra sauce and sides?" she asked. Her face looked animated.

"Sure." He signaled for the waitress to come to the table. Pussy ordered their food and asked for the dessert menu. When he turned back to her, he saw her panicking.

"Crap, I'm so sorry. I don't have any money. There's no way for me to pay you back."

"Don't worry about it, baby. I've never taken a woman out with the intention of her paying. This is all on me, so enjoy it." He took hold of her hand once again.

Pussy liked the feel of her hand in his. There was no way he'd be giving Sasha back to Kenneth, knowing about what he'd done. The club wouldn't let a woman go back to someone who was going to hurt her.

Sasha was vulnerable.

"I'm sorry about your friend," Sasha said, breaking the silence that had fallen between them.

"Thank you. Ashley, she was a spitfire and didn't deserve to die." He stopped talking to clear his throat.

"Have you killed someone before?" she asked.

"I'm not going to answer that."

"I don't know what else to talk to you about. I hate silence."

"Tell me what you know about our club." He ignored all the other people in the steakhouse. The smells were making him desperate for food.

"I don't know anything about you. My mom and Kenneth have warned me to stay away from you. They've not said anything other than that you're dangerous."

"And yet, you're not afraid of me?" he asked.

Looking down her body, he caught sight of her hardened nipples. Did he turn Sasha on?

She's blind, you idiot. Don't start thinking about that shit.

"No. You don't make me feel afraid. I've been around Kenneth. He's not a nice guy. Whenever he goes to town he's always in meetings with an Italian guy."

He paused. "Italian guy?"

"I think he's an Italian. He's got an accent, but I think I've heard Kenneth say he's not actually Italian. I think he has mixed Spanish and Italian heritage, but I'm not sure."

"What does he look like?" he asked.

"I don't fucking know. Blind remember?"

"Shit, sorry." Could Kenneth be working for Frederick? Shit, today was only supposed to be about getting out of Piston County.

****

Sasha smiled. Did he know how sweet he was?

"You've no need to be sorry. A lot of people forget about it, even my mom." She tried her best to reassure him.

"It doesn't matter. You shouldn't have to go through something like that. It's not right."

She really wished she knew what he looked like. From being next to him, she knew he was tall. Was he taller than Kenneth? She didn't know. In her mind she pictured Pussy with messy blond hair, which he never brushed. Bed hair, she believed they called it. He had to have tattoos. Every biker had to have them. She wondered what pictures or words they wore.

"Why do you go by Pussy and not Shane?" she asked.

"You're a curious little devil, aren't you?"

"I've got a lot of things in life to be curious about. You intrigue me." She rested her face on her hand, wondering if she was even meeting his eyes. Did he have brown, ocean blue, green, or hazel colored eyes?

There was so much she wanted to know about him.

"I intrigue you?"

"Yeah. I've heard how bikers are supposed to be rough, tough, and mean, yet I think you're sweet, possibly the sweetest man I've ever known," she said, smiling.

He made a gagging sound. "Babe, don't go around telling people I'm sweet. I'll lose my reputation."

She giggled as something was placed on the table. Pulling back, she squeezed her hands together to help ground her. Sudden noise always alarmed her.

"I hope you enjoy your food," the woman said.

Was the waitress eyeing Pussy up?

"Thanks, doll," Pussy said. Seconds passed, and Sasha tried to hear everything she could.

"Noise and movement around you unnerve you, don't they?" he asked.

He touched her hand and slowly slid her fingers over the plate. "This is the burger. Let me know when you want it. Here are some fries."

There he was again being all sweet with her food. "Erm, thank you. Yes, sudden movement or noise upsets me. I don't know what's going on, and not being able to see freaks me out," she said.

Silence fell once again. She picked up a couple of fries and started to eat.

"Why are you not freaking out more about your condition?" he asked.

"I've had it over four years. It's hard to freak out anymore. I just get frustrated about what I can and can't do." She stopped talking to eat.

"Is it permanent?" Pussy asked.

"In the beginning the doctors were unsure, as with all trauma it carries risks. Now, I'm permanent. I'll never be able to see again. I think they said there was too much damage to my nerves or something. I was still reeling from being told I would never see again. I didn't pay much attention." She'd gotten used to not being able to see. There was still a tiny spark of hope that maybe one day that would all change, or at least some new wonder drug or maybe even surgery would change it. She didn't expect it to. "Could you pass me my burger?"

"Sure." He placed the burger in her hands.

"This is huge."

"It won't be the only thing you think is huge." The words came out as a mumble, but she caught them.

"What do you mean?" she asked.

"Do you have a boyfriend?"

"No. Stepdad keeps all men away." She took a bite of the burger and moaned. "This is amazing."

"I'm not taking you back to your stepfather."

She paused with the burger pressed to her lips. "What?"

"You heard me. I'm not taking you back there."

Keeping hold of her burger, she lowered it down. "You can't do that."

"Not only am I going to do that, but you're not going to stop me."

"You'll be making a mistake," she said. Inside she was cheering at having a savior intent on helping her. No one would try to take her away from Kenneth. Would she finally be able to break free from the cycle her stepfather had forced her into?

"You expect me to feed you and drop you back at the diner back in Piston County for that fucker to take you, knowing that he hurt you?"

"You sound angry?"

"I'm pissed, Sasha. Don't you have any urge to protect yourself?"

"Yes, but you don't know what he's like."

She jerked as he touched her arm.

"Don't be afraid, Sasha. The club will take care of you."

"Why?"

"Because I'd ask them to take care of you. They'll do what I ask."

"None of this makes any sense to me. I don't think we should be talking about this. Crap, I don't know what I'm doing."

She dropped the burger.

"It's on the plate." He caught both of her hands within his. "Stop freaking out."

Sasha stopped even as her heart pounded inside her chest. What was she supposed to do?

"Where would I go?" she asked. "I didn't want for this to happen."

"You need to stop worrying about what could happen and start thinking about yourself, babe. You're twenty years old, living at home because that fucker blinded you. I'm offering you an out."

Biting her lip, she tried to focus on everything that happened. For the last four years she'd tried to believe the story of herself falling downstairs rather than remembering the feel of Kenneth hurting her. Her mother had begged her not to say anything, asking for her trust. What the hell was she supposed to do?

"He'll hurt my mother. I can't leave her alone."

She was breaking inside. How long had she been with Pussy? Was it already too late to get back to the diner before Kenneth saw she left? She didn't want anything to happen to her mother because of her.

Do you really want to leave?

No, she didn't want to leave, and the thought of going back to Piston County filled her with dread. Pussy was offering her an out, and she wasn't even taking it.

"Then let me deal with him, Sasha. I don't care what he does to me. I will not leave you alone with him." His grip tightened on her arm. It wasn't painful or threatening. He held her tightly, and it kept her grounded. She could think past the fear.

"Okay."

"Are you sure?"

"No, I'm not sure. I'm not sure of anything right now. We were only supposed to be having lunch."

Her hands shook. She felt the tremors.

"Stop worrying."

"I can't help it. Is this what you do with all the women you take out to dinner?" she asked.

"No. Most of the women end up in my bed and I eat out their pussy."

She gasped. "What?"

"You heard me, Sasha."

"You eat out women's pussies? Is that some kind of carnivore reference?" She frowned. Pussy didn't sound like the kind of person to eat people, let alone women. Was eating out pussy porn or something?

"You're a virgin?" he asked.

"It's not hard to guess that I am. I've never been around enough men to want to sleep with me."

Silence met her words.

"Have I said the wrong words?"

"I want to fuck you," he said.

She licked her lips. "Did I hear you correctly?"

Squeezing her legs together, she tried to relieve the ache that was building inside her.

"Yes, you heard me correctly."

"Wow, this conversation has changed tack. One moment we're talking about killing people, then Kenneth, now sex." She liked talking a lot more than she liked silence. There were times when she was home that she'd lie down on her bed, listening to classical music, anything to stop herself from listening to the silence, knowing there was nothing she could do about it.

Pussy chuckled.

"So the, erm, eating pussy reference was about sex, not eating people?"

His chuckle turned into a full blown laugh. "Babe, you're cracking me up. You really are completely innocent."

"I went blind before I could look porn up on the 'net. They don't exactly have sex books in Braille for me to read."

He stopped laughing, and the moment he did, she missed the sound.

"You don't have to stop laughing. It's funny, even if I don't know what you're laughing at." She shrugged, offering him a smile.

"You've got the prettiest, sweetest smile I've ever seen," he said, catching her off guard.

"Thank you."

"Shit, I'm turning into a pussy now. Fuck, no, why don't you listen to books? They do them on audio now or so I've heard."

She shook her head. "All purchases have to go through Kenneth. He won't let me have books."

Pussy still held onto her arms.

"I'm getting hungry again. Can I finish eating my food?" She didn't want him to let her go, but she didn't have a choice.

"Sure." He gave her back her burger, and they started eating.

Her curiosity built inside her as he stopped talking and ate.

"What is it like?" she asked.

"Eating pussy?" Her cheeks had to be bright red. They were hot to the touch. Her curiosity was going to get her in a lot of trouble one day, if it hadn't already.

"I don't know what it's like. I've never had a pussy to be eaten."

She giggled, shaking her head. "You're making this harder for me."

"No, baby, I'm making sure you know that I eat pussy. I don't have one."

"Okay. I knew that."

"Baby, eat your burger and then we'll talk more when I get you safe."

She wanted to argue, but what more could she say? Pussy was the one in control of this conversation, not her.

Chapter Four

Staring up at the sky, Pussy knew he needed to make a call to Devil and his brothers. Glancing behind him, he saw Sasha still remained on the bench where he'd put her drinking her milkshake. From the steakhouse, he rode for the next hour to try to clear his head. With Sasha's legs cradling his body, he'd not been able to think at all. Shit, Devil was going to be completely pissed with him.

Now was not the time to start a fight with one of the men in town who could cause them a lot of problems. Pulling out his cell phone, he saw over ten missed calls from the clubhouse alone. Shit, Kenneth must have seen Sasha was missing.

He couldn't send her back to the bastard who hurt her. There was no way he'd do it, not even if Devil ordered him to.

His cell phone went off. Keeping his gaze on Sasha, he accepted the call.

"Where the fuck have you been?" Devil asked, his voice raised to a shout. "We've had the fucking cops around here looking for you. Rumor is you've stolen a woman, Kenneth Carmichael's blind, fucking stepdaughter. What the fuck have you got to say about that?"

Pussy went to open his mouth. Devil didn't give him chance to respond.

"I told you to stay out of fucking sight. We need to stay clean and you go off with a woman who can put you in fucking jail."

"She's twenty, boss. The girl I'm with is twenty, and the guy who's so concerned about her, caused her to be fucking blind." Pussy glanced back up at the sky. Maybe going straight to heaven or hell would be better than facing his president.

"You're certain."

"I'm not sending her back to Piston County to the fucker who hurt her. If this was Lexie, you would have done the same, or to Judi."

Devil cursed. "Fuck, why can't we ever do shit that's simple?"

"I think The Skulls are cursed. Ever since we started to visit them, our lives have turned to shit."

"Shut up," Devil yelled.

Pussy winced, moving the phone away from his ear.

"I think for tonight it would be best if you checked into a hotel or something. Don't come back here today. It's only going to cause problems."

"Will do."

"Is this what I think it is?" Devil asked.

"I don't know. What do you think it is?" Pussy tried to be vague in his response.

"Are you going to fuck this girl? Turn her into your old lady?" Devil sounded tired once again. The shit with Gonzalez was really starting to wear thin.

"I can't answer that right now, boss. She means something."

"You want to fuck her?"

"Yeah."

"Then this is going to start causing problems," Devil said.

"I've wanted to fuck other women before. None of them have ever been a problem."

"Are you being fucking stupid on purpose? None of the other women you've fucked have forced you to take this next step. You took this girl—"

"Woman," Pussy said, interrupting Devil's rant.

"Don't fucking interrupt me. This *girl*, you've

taken her away from her family and telling me you're not letting her back to the people who can protect her? Please, tell me, Pussy, if that's not laying fucking claim to her, what is?"

He remained silent, seeing Devil's logic.

Watching her suck on the straw of her milkshake sent Pussy's cock into overdrive. Fuck, this woman didn't have a clue how hot she was.

"Are you going to answer me?"

"Yeah, I'm laying claim to her. There's something else that you might want to get Whizz to have a look at."

"What is it now?" Devil asked.

"I was talking with Sasha, and she mentioned that her stepfather Kenneth was having meetings with an Italian guy. She can't give us anything more as she can't see."

"What's this got to do with anything? Whizz is busy as it is trying to find ways of bringing Gonzalez down."

Running fingers through his hair, Pussy watched a couple of men staring at his woman. Starting toward her, he spoke quickly.

"An Italian in meetings with one of the men on the town council, Devil. That strikes me as odd, especially with Gonzalez throwing his weight around. It's too much of a coincidence not to think of the two together," Pussy said.

The two men saw him and moved in the opposite direction. Sasha didn't give any notice of him being closer to her. She looked happy. Every now and then she'd smile and look up to the sky. She took his breath away with her openness of enjoying life. How much had Kenneth taken from her? He didn't think the bastard had raped her or touched her, but he couldn't be sure of anything.

"Fuck, you're right. I'll get Whizz looking into everything. This shit is really starting to bug me. Stay out of town tonight and we'll deal with the other shit tomorrow morning. Make sure your woman is on board with whatever plan you've got in place."

"Will do. Let me know if Whizz finds anything out. I don't want to be kept waiting."

Devil agreed before hanging up.

"Hey, babe."

She turned her head and stared at his stomach. "Hey, is everything okay?"

"Yeah, how's your milkshake?"

"Good. Do you want some?"

Sasha offered up some shake for him.

"No, I'm good."

He took a seat beside her on the bench. "Wow, you seem a little put out. Did your phone call not go so well?" she asked.

"We can't go back to Piston County tonight. Your stepfather caused a few problems. We'll wait 'til tomorrow and I'll take you back."

"No, you're going to have to take me back. I don't want you getting into trouble."

"I won't. My president has given me some orders, and there's nothing we can do. We've got to do as he asked."

"President? None of this makes any sense. I'm freaking out."

"Do you trust me?" he asked.

"Yes."

He held her arm so she wouldn't hurt herself. "Then let me take care of you."

He reached out to cup her cheek. She didn't jerk away from him or tense up. Stroking her pale cheek, he held back a groan. His Sasha was smooth to the touch.

"Why would you want to?" she asked.

"I don't know." Closing the distance, Pussy stared at her lips. Fuck, they were red, plump, and in need of kissing.

Slamming his lips down on hers, he moaned the instant they touched. She whimpered. Her hand cupped the back of his hand, caressing down to his cheek.

He slid his tongue along her lips waiting for her to open up. Sasha didn't keep him waiting long.

She tasted of the chocolate milkshake she'd been drinking. Their moans mingled together. Tilting her head back, he deepened the kiss. When their lips touching wasn't enough, he picked her up getting her to straddle his hips. Her pussy pressed against his cock. Their clothing stopped him from going any further, but he wanted to. Pussy didn't want to stop feeling her ride his cock.

Groaning, he slid his tongue in and out of her mouth, mimicking fucking her.

"Pussy?" She whispered his name against his lips.

"What, baby?"

"What's happening? I don't know what's going on."

Pulling away from her lips, he pressed his head to hers. "We're going to have to stop. I'm going to take you to a hotel room where we're going to have a really long discussion."

If he was in luck, he'd find a place to get some condoms. His cock ached from the feel of her body alone.

"Something's wrong," she said, moaning. She thrust against him, rubbing her pussy against his shaft. Sasha caught his face, kissing his lips. "Please, make it stop aching."

He groaned as she dry fucked him on the bench.

You caused this, so now you've got to finish it.

Picking her up, he walked her back until she was next to his bike. Glancing behind him, he made sure no one could see what he was doing. Sliding his palm down the front of her body, he moaned. She really was nicely rounded in all the right places.

"What are you doing?" she asked.

"I'm going to make you feel good. Relax, and this will go well." Fingering the button of her jeans, he found there was enough space for him to slide his hand inside. Down he went until he cupped her pussy. Her panties were soaking wet. Sliding them aside, he fingered her slit. She was so turned on.

Sasha gripped his arms tightly, groaning. "That feels so good."

"It's going to feel much better, baby, I promise you."

"How can it feel better?" She stopped, letting out a moan. Before she could finish, Pussy claimed her lips. He didn't want anyone else hearing her scream out her pleasure. Her cries of release were for him and him alone.

When they were alone she could scream until her heart's content, but until then, she would be silent.

Stroking two fingers over her clit, he slammed his tongue inside her mouth. She opened up to him, no longer fighting. She thrust against his fingers, whimpering, crying out, and moaning whenever he released her lips long enough to hear.

Within seconds she was screaming out her release. Her whole body shook at the sudden burst of pleasure pulsing from her. Banding an arm around her waist, he continued to stroke her. Sasha begged him to stop. Kissing her head, he withdrew his hand, and sucked the cream from his fingers.

"Fuck me, baby, you taste so fucking good." He let out a moan as her essence filled his mouth. Swallowing down the taste of her, he knew once was never going to be enough for him.

"Wow," she said.

"Come on. Let me find a hotel and I can make you feel that way again." Helping her onto the back of his bike, Pussy struggled to get comfortable. His dick threatened to split his trousers open he was so hard.

Sasha was proving to be as much trouble as he imagined.

****

When he pulled out of the food court or wherever he'd gotten the milkshake from, Sasha had been reeling from what she'd experienced. Pussy had just given her, her first orgasm. What was she supposed to do or say? No one had prepared her for this in life.

Her mother didn't talk about sex, and Sasha never asked questions. She didn't know how long they rode for. The time passed, and all she could think about was the feel of his fingers down her pants.

Get a grip.

Trying to push her thoughts aside was difficult. The threat of Kenneth couldn't even stop her feelings. None of it made any sense to her.

Time passed, and the bike finally came to a stop. "Where are we?" she asked.

"Don't worry about it. I'm not going to leave you on your own." He helped her off the bike, removed the helmet, and took her hand. She followed behind him with sure steps. This was the first time she'd ever been out walking when she was sure the person wouldn't hurt her or cause her to fall. Kenneth always found ways of making her feel unsure on her feet.

He opened the door, and she reached out instinctively to put her hand on it. Other times, Kenneth made sure she hurt herself.

Stop thinking about him. He's not here to take this from you.

Blowing out a breath, she stopped as Pussy placed a palm on her stomach. Was he purposefully giving her independence?

She didn't know. Pussy didn't seem the guy to go out of his way for a girl. Were they all throwing themselves at him?

"Hey, darling. We're looking for a room for the night," Pussy said.

The hand holding hers released her. She panicked for a split second then released a sigh as he placed that arm along her shoulders.

"For you and your sister?" the woman asked.

"Nah, babe, this is my woman. We're having a little fun before duty calls back at home." Pussy kissed her temple.

"We don't do rooms by the hour."

How dare the bitch say something so mean? Sasha went to speak up, but Pussy got there before her.

"Get your fucking manager before you seriously piss me the fuck off, bitch." Pussy had never once talked to her like that.

Licking her lips, Sasha felt nervous for the girl. "I'm sorry."

"I don't care to hear what you've got to say. Get your fucking manager and you better hope he or she is feeling in a forgiving mood."

Minutes passed, and she didn't hear anything else. "Don't you think you were a little hard on her?" Sasha asked.

"Bitch was insulting, and I don't accept crap like

that when it comes to you." He kissed her head again. "Don't panic or anything. I want a room, and I want it without attitude."

When the manager arrived, Sasha tucked herself against Pussy. Was he frightening to look at when he was angry? She didn't think of him as scary. Tuning out what he was saying, she closed her eyes and inhaled the scent of him.

What if you could see?

She'd long given up that hope. Right now, she didn't need to see with his arms wrapped around her. Pussy made her feel protected. She knew it was wrong, but she adored his name. Everything about him contradicted what Kenneth wanted for her.

Pussy was a hard, rough biker with a startling sweet side.

"I expect a fucking discount for her treatment."

"Absolutely. Here, take this room. It's a beautiful room, and if you need any help at all, let me know." She assumed that was the manager stumbling over his words.

"Come on, baby. Let's get out of here."

Pussy led her out of the room. She went with him.

"Right, we're going to go up some steps. Are you good to make them?"

"Yes."

They took several steps forward, and Pussy paused. "Step."

She searched for the step and started the momentum going up. Pussy's arms on her waist kept her steady. Making her way up the flight of stairs was a huge achievement for her. Smiling at the top, she giggled. "I did it."

"What's the matter, baby?"

"At home they installed one of those chairs for me to get to my room. That was my first flight of steps, and I did it." She flung her arms around him, holding on tight.

Pussy laughed with her. She wanted to share this enjoyment with him.

"He's really kept you trapped."

Sasha stopped to think about what he said. He was right. Kenneth had kept her trapped, afraid to move to the outside world. What could he hope to achieve with keeping her around?

"Yes, he has."

"Baby, don't worry about him. He's never going to hurt you."

"How do you know that?"

"Chaos Bleeds, we're a family as much as we're a club. We won't let anything happen to you. I promise."

Could she accept his help?

Did she have a choice?

Her mother couldn't stop what Kenneth had done.

"I don't want to talk about him anymore. He's ruined my life enough." She'd barely lived. All of her friends were off having a great time while she stayed at home, waiting to live. Slowly, she was being beat down, and having Pussy for company was showing her that.

He took hold of her hand and led her down toward the room. She didn't try to steady herself like normal. Sasha trusted him to get her to where he wanted her safely.

She listened for the click of the lock.

"Right, we're here." Pussy opened the door and helped her inside.

"Is it dark or light out?"

"It's getting dark." He flicked the light on.

"I wouldn't worry about it. It doesn't matter if it's light or dark." She tried to smile. Did he like the way she looked? For four years she'd not looked in a mirror. Was she pretty? He had to like her to get her off, right? "I'm so confused," she said.

"Baby, talk to me, and I might be able to help with that confusion." He ran his hands up and down her arms, comforting her.

"No, I can't ask you this. It's crazy, and I'm sure women's magazines would be against me asking something like this," she said.

Pussy chuckled. "Just ask."

Letting out a sigh, she nibbled on her lip. "Okay, do you find me attractive?" she asked.

"Baby, you've got no idea how hot you make me. You're so fucking perfect and beautiful. You put other women to shame."

She smiled. "Really?"

"Does this feel like I want to fuck something ugly?" He placed her hand on the hard ridge of his cock. *Wow.* No, it didn't feel like he wanted to fuck something ugly. "This is what you do to me."

His other hand went underneath her chin, tilting her head back. She didn't know what she was looking at. This was what she hated the most, the lack of knowing where her gaze fell.

"I like what I do to you," she said.

"I'm going to kiss you now."

Did he want her to say anything or to deny him? She wanted to feel his lips on hers.

He moved some of her hair out of the way, and then his mouth was on hers. At first they were gentle, exploring hers. His tongue glided over her lips, and she moaned at the smallest contact.

"You taste so fucking good," he said, muttering the words against her.

"Please don't stop." She needed his lips on hers. There was no way she'd be able to survive without his kiss.

Pussy plundered her mouth, and she whimpered.

"Yes, that's it, baby. Kiss me back." He stroked his tongue along her own, and she met him stroke for stroke, tasting him. She loved the feel of him and the way he licked along her lips before going inside. He broke the kiss first, kissing down her neck.

You don't know him.

She didn't know him, yet her body was more than happy to have him touching her.

"Let's get rid of this jacket and make you a little more comfortable." He pushed her jacket from her shoulders, and she heard it fall to the floor. With her arms free, she wrapped them around his body, rubbing herself against him.

"Fuck, baby, you make me want to do crazy shit to keep you." He cupped her cheeks, turning her head this way and that. She couldn't fight him or her body. For once she craved to do something that would make her feel good and no one else.

His lips moved down to her collarbone. His tongue slid over her pulse. The shirt she wore stopped him from going any further.

"You're going to have to tell me to stop, Sasha. I want you, and if you let me, I'll fuck you all night long and show you what you've been missing," he said.

Chapter Five

Pussy waited patiently for her to respond. The light was on, and it was almost nightfall outside. His cock was causing him some problems, he was so hard. Gritting his teeth, he continued to wait for her response.

"I don't want you to stop."

Her eyes were on his chest. Could it be possible for her to see him one day? Pussy didn't know the answer, and he didn't care. He'd have her any way he could get her.

"I'll take it slow. I know this is your first time."

"Are you going to eat my pussy?" she asked. Her cheeks were a lovely shade of red. He wondered what he could do to her in order to have her all a nice shade of red.

Removing his jacket, he threw it to the bed. Taking his cell phone out of his pocket, he turned it off so he wouldn't be called away from taking time with her body.

"What are you doing?"

During the hours they were together, he'd noticed she hated silence. She'd ask questions or say stuff to fill in any gaps.

"I'm turning my phone off. I don't want the club interrupting me. Tonight is all about you, and if I have to answer my phone, then it stops being about you and all about them."

"I wouldn't mind, if you had to answer the call."

"When I start eating your pussy, Sasha, I'm not going to want to stop." He gave her his full attention. "Now, I'm going to ask you one more time, do you want to do this?

She stayed still for the longest time, frowning. How could she not see? Her eyes were filled with so much emotion, and yet she didn't even know what he looked like.

"Yes, I want to do this." She started to fumble with her shirt. Reaching out, he placed his palm over her shaking hands, and she immediately stopped.

"There's no rush for us to do anything," he said. *Stop it, you fucking idiot. You want her. Stop giving her reasons not to want you.*

"Pussy, I want this. Please, I've spent the last four years feeling like I can't do anything. Don't take away the few hours of pleasure you've promised me."

"You're a virgin," he said.

What the fuck are you doing?

"You're not. You know what you're doing. Can't you take the lead and do what you always do with women?" she asked.

He didn't want to treat her like he did other women.

Stop being a pussy and give her what she wants.

Fisting his palms at his side, he reached out to cup her face.

"I only ask one thing," she said.

"What is it?" he asked.

"Talk to me all the way through. I hate silence, and it makes me nervous."

Pussy smiled. "You want me to talk dirty to you."

"Yes. Tell me what you're doing."

"I can do that, baby." He tugged off his shirt. Taking hold of her hand, he pressed her palm to his chest. "I've taken my shirt off. You can touch me now and feel how naked I am."

He watched her lick her lips.

"Do you have tattoos?" she asked.

"Yeah."

"Tell me about them."

Taking hold of her hand, he pushed her palm up to his left arm. "I've got the Chaos Bleeds symbol here. It's a skull-and-crossbones, metallic in appearance. Quite a few of the guys have this symbol on their bodies." Down he went to around his wrist. "I thought it was ironic to have a pair of cuffs inked around my wrists. I'm not held by the law, but I'm held by my club. I'd do anything for them."

"Even go to prison."

"Sasha, I'd die for the club, that's how serious this commitment is."

"Would they do the same for you?" she asked.

"Yes, they would."

"How can you be so sure?"

"I know my club. We've been through a lot together to get here. They wouldn't stop there if they didn't have to." He let her stroke the inside of his wrists. Pussy refused to think about why. The feel of her fingers lightly touching his skin made him feel alive in ways he didn't think was possible, especially to him. For so long he'd been taking his pleasure from endless women without any care for them. He cared what Sasha felt.

With her first time, he wished to make it as memorable as possible.

Be real, you don't want any other man to touch what's yours.

In such a short space of time Sasha had gone from being "the blind girl" to someone more. Devil was right. He'd never gone to this much trouble for anyone else, not even Lexie or Ashley.

"What other ink do you have?" she asked.

He took her hand and slowly stroked over the top part of his body going from arm to arm, across his chest then over his stomach. She didn't say anything, only smiled every now and then when he pointed out certain marks on his body.

"I've got some on my back as well."

"Can I feel?"

"Sure." He turned around, and she followed the movement with her palm. Her fingers touched his skin ever so lightly. "I've got a lion on my back along with several other mini tattoos. There's a tiny butterfly across my right shoulder because I lost a fucking bet, and I'm never going to live it down as long as I live."

She giggled. Pussy liked the feel of her hands on his body. There was something electrifying about how she touched him. She was gentle, never rough. He wanted to show her how rough she could be with him. Pussy loved the feel of a woman's nails raking the skin as she screamed in orgasm. In Chaos Bleeds he was the star of making a woman feel good.

"I wish I could see them. You feel like you work out. Do you?"

"I work out as much as I can."

Her hands danced along his skin. "It must be nice."

"What?"

"To be able to work out without fear of falling or bumping into things. It has been so long since I've felt like that."

Turning around he saw the smile dancing across her lips.

"I can help you with that."

"Is this another thing the club does? Feel sorry for other women who can't do stuff themselves?" she asked.

"No, this is all me. I want you to feel good about yourself. You shouldn't have to rely on anyone."

The smile dropped from her lips again. "I don't want to depend on anyone. It sucks. I always wish there was something more I could do."

Cupping her cheek, he ran his thumb along her bottom lip. "Baby, there's always something you can do, and I'm going to be here to see that you do get the chance to do what you want. I hate people who hurt others."

"I don't want to talk about them anymore."

"Good, because I don't want to hear what any of those fuckers have to say about you. After today, Kenneth will never be able to touch you."

Pussy didn't care about his connection with Gonzalez. Anyone who hurt a woman and took away her sight was someone who needed to be taken out in Pussy's book.

"You're one of a kind," she said.

"And I've not even gotten my mouth on your pussy. You're going to be a lucky woman soon," he said, winking at her.

She chuckled, and she'd not even seen him wink.

"You've not had a lot to laugh about lately, have you?" he asked.

"No, I've not, but you're about to change that for me." Her hands were laid on his arms, waiting.

"Yes, I'm about to change all of that for you." Tilting her head back, he stared at her face. The trust she showed him scared the shit out of him. She should be more cautious. He'd killed a lot of men, caused problems wherever he went, and done it all with a smile and in the name of the club. There was nothing he wouldn't do for the club.

Even as he looked at her and thought how she deserved a better man, he didn't want to miss this opportunity.

"I'm going to kiss you now," he said.

She whimpered but still didn't pull away. Dropping his head down, he brushed his lips against hers.

Sasha melted against him and he gave everything to her. Plunging his tongue inside her mouth, he moaned, going in deep. He glided his tongue over hers, going as deep as he could for her to take as much of him as possible.

"You don't have a clue what you're doing to me, do you?" he asked, muttering the words against her lips.

Shaking her head, she ran her hands up his arms to band around his neck. Sliding his hands to her waist, he fingered the flesh that was revealed by her shirt being ridden up. She was soft against his hardness. Moaning, he licked along her lips then pressed kisses down her face to her neck. She moved her head to the side giving him better access to kiss her.

"You're going to drive me insane," he said, moaning. Her fingers tightened in the hair at the base of his neck.

Going under her shirt, he touched her skin and felt her shake beneath his touch.

She's innocent. Take your time and go as slow as possible.

Closing his eyes, he tried to consider her innocence as he touched her.

Take her.

"Let me know if I'm going too fast for you," he said.

"You're not going fast enough, Pussy. Please, I ache all over again." Sasha took over, pressing her lips to his. He was so close that she didn't miss him as she kissed him back.

Wrapping his arms around her, he took her back until they were closer to the bed. He needed the flat surface in case he lost his mind and took her there in the center of the room.

"I'm going to take your shirt off," he said.

In one sweep, he removed her shirt leaving her in

a simple cotton bra. The underwear was unattractive, yet it didn't detract from the beauty of her pale skin.

"What's the matter? You stopped and didn't say anything."

"You're beautiful. Your bra doesn't do you justice, but it doesn't matter." He fingered the strap then ran the pads of his fingers across her chest to the top of her breasts. "I'm honored that you've picked me." He slid the strap of her bra down her arm.

He noticed the goosebumps that erupted all over her arms.

"Are you still with me?"

"Keep talking and I'm more than with you."

Pussy chuckled.

Turning her around, he flicked the catch of her bra. "Don't stop it from falling. I want to see your tits," he said, whispering the words against her head.

"You really are sinful, aren't you?"

"We've not even gotten started on the good stuff yet. Give me chance to show you how good I can make this." He eased the bra off her arms and simply gasped. Her tits were everything he'd thought they would be. They were large and beautiful with tight red nipples. Licking his lips, he reached out and cupped her breast. Sliding his thumb across the tip he watched her gasp. Her breasts were sensitive to the slightest touch. "Do you like that?"

"Yes. Please, don't stop."

"I've got more exciting stuff to do to you." Moving to the next breast, he circled the nipple. She pushed her chest out toward him, offering her body up for him to play with.

Feeling wicked, he claimed one of her nipples with his lips, sucking the hard bud into his mouth.

She cried out. Her hands went to his arms with

her nails sinking inside his flesh. Pinching the other breast, he stared up her body to see her response.

Her eyes were closed, and her mouth was open slightly. She looked amazed by what he was doing. Going to the second breast, he teased it as much as the first. With his free hand Pussy fingered the button of her jeans. Moving from one breast to the other, he took his time, loving her tits. Her tits deserved the time to be sucked, nibbled, and adored.

Opening the button of her jeans, he popped them open and slid the zipper down. Cupping her hips, he pushed her jeans down her thighs. She wiggled, helping him push the offending item of clothing down.

Releasing her breasts, he sank down in front of her. He placed his hands on her hips so she knew where he was.

"I'm going to take off your pants."

"Don't let go," she said, biting her lip.

"I won't, baby, I promise."

"You make a lot of promises." She let out a breath.

He didn't respond and started to peel her panties away from her. Pubic hair covered her pussy, obscuring her from his view. When he was close to a razor he'd be trimming her hair so he could see the lips of her sex.

She smelled feminine and sweet.

"You're not talking. Is something wrong?" she asked.

"No, nothing is wrong." He let go of her hip and started to slide his fingers through her hair. "I want to remove some of this hair when I get my hands on a razor. Will you let me?"

"Yes, if you promise not to cut me."

"Don't you know by now that I'll take care of all of your needs?" He returned his grip to her hip and walked her back. Once the backs of her knees hit the bed she sat down. "Actually, will you trust me to go and get that razor? I don't want to leave you alone, but I also want you to feel everything I can do to you."

"You want to leave?" she asked.

"I'll be back. I'll lock the door, and all you have to do is sit here and wait. There's a shop down the street, and I forgot to get rubbers, babe. I can't fuck you without a condom. You could get pregnant." He groaned, dropping his head onto her leg. "Fuck, you make me want you so much that I've forgot to get condoms."

She chuckled. "Okay, erm, could I lie on the bed while you're gone?"

"Sure."

He helped her onto the bed then kissed her lips. "I'll be back before you know it."

****

Sasha heard the door go and then silence. "That's it, he's gone. He's gone, and I'm lying on a bed talking to myself because I'm going insane. No one is here, and I've got nothing to say."

Running her hands across the bedding she tried to bring some focus to her little world. One morning with Pussy and she'd left Piston County behind. Had Pussy claimed her? She didn't understand what any of this meant. Holding her hands in front of her, she thought about the feel of his body underneath his touch. He'd been hard, each ridge of his muscles outlined against her palm.

Silence filled the gap in between her talking. She hated this. If she had her sight she'd be able to watch television or sit beside the window looking out at the night. Her vision was a constant, never ending night.

Would he come back?

Over the years Kenneth had made her believe that

she was a nuisance. Even her own mother didn't want to know her. Her mother spent most of her time at the bottom of a bottle or throwing down some pills rather than spend time with her. Every now and then, the old mother she knew would appear with food and conversation. Whatever Kenneth said was a lie.

Push them aside. Stop thinking about either of them. They're nothing right now.

She did her best to ignore them and focused on the silence that surrounded her. In no time at all, the door was opening. "I've got the stuff I need, baby."

The door closed, and more shuffling happened.

"Shit, I should have left the television on, shouldn't I? Fuck. I'm so sorry."

Sasha giggled. "You don't have to keep apologizing. I'm more than capable of looking after myself. I didn't get into any trouble lying here."

"Still, I'm going to have to learn to take care of you."

The bed dipped, and she let out a yelp. "Fuck, I'm just sitting beside you."

She nodded, reaching out but coming against air.

"Here, I'm here." Pussy took hold of her hand and placed it on his body.

"You're there." She touched his body and frowned. "You're naked?"

"I didn't have time to put clothes on. I wanted to get the stuff and get back to you. I forgot to put a shirt on. It doesn't matter. The guy at the store didn't charge me much. I think he was too busy ogling my hot bod," he said.

Chuckling, she squeezed his arm. She really did love the feel of his skin in her hands, and she told him so.

"See, you only want me for my body," Pussy said.

"No, I want you for more." She did her best to smile.

"I'm going to kiss you now." The bed creaked under his weight.

"Okay."

His fingers slid over her cheek, and his palm went to the pillow at the side of her head. At first his lips grazed hers, showing her where he was. "I'm close to you now." His tongue caressed her lips, and she opened her mouth.

Meeting his tongue with her own, she kissed him deeply. Circling his neck, she moaned as his body pressed to her front. His chest grazed her nipples. Crying out, she held onto him, never wanting to let him go.

"Fuck, I've never felt this way from a fucking kiss," he said, muttering the words against hers.

"I love you kissing me."

Pussy tensed. "What?"

"I like when you kiss me," she said. What was wrong with what she said?

"Good."

You said the love word. Men hate the love word. Don't say it again.

"I'm going to get some water," he said, releasing her.

He moved away from her, and she was alone again. She heard him moving around.

"Are you in the bathroom?" she asked.

"Yes. I'm going to trim your pubic hair."

"That's very clinical." No one had touched her between her thighs. Pussy was the only man to get this close to her, and she wasn't going to let anyone else near her. The only person she wanted was Pussy. If she'd had her sight, she wouldn't have stayed at home. She knew in her heart she wouldn't have let her mother get this bad.

Some way she'd have put a stop to it. In the back of her mind she couldn't help but feel let down by her mother. She shouldn't have to take care of her mother.

More movement reached her ears as he put stuff down.

"I'm just putting this bowl on the drawer beside the bed."

"I'm sorry I said love. It was stupid of me."

He chuckled. "Took me by surprise, babe. Never had a woman say she loved something I did. They've enjoyed what I do but never loved it."

"Are you trying to make me jealous?" she asked. A jolt of pain went straight through her heart at the mention of the other women in his life. Why did he have to be so mean?

Get up and leave.

She didn't want to. Sasha wanted to know what he could do to her.

"No, I'm not trying to do anything. I'm just being an ass." He cupped her cheek. "I'm new at this."

"New at what?"

"Caring. I'm not used to caring. I never usually have to care about anyone or anything," he said.

"Do you care about me?"

"Yes, I do. I care more than I like to." His thumb stroked her bottom lip. "I'm going to be using a razor and some scissors. Please be still."

"Then talk to me. It helps to calm me when I hear you talk."

"I'll remember that, baby."

She licked her lips and waited. The bed dipped under his weight. He placed something beside her hip. Pussy opened her thighs. She went to close her thighs but stopped herself.

He needs to get to you.

"Good girl," he said.

"I'm not used to this."

"It's okay. I don't expect you to be used to this. You're innocent." Pussy's palm landed on the inside of her thigh. "I'm going to start trimming in a second. I've got a towel here. Lift your ass up," he said.

She lifted her ass up, and when he placed a palm on her stomach, pushing her back down, she relaxed. The towel was soft underneath her ass.

"This is the strangest thing I've ever done."

"I've never done this before. This is a new experience for the pair of us," he said.

"If you've never done this before, should I trust you near me?"

He chuckled. "This is going to take some getting used to."

"What?"

"Talking all the way through what I'm doing."

"Do you want me to shut up?" she asked.

"No, I actually like to hear you talking. Strange, huh? I'm used to hating a woman talk."

She let out a growl. "You're going to drive me insane with your sexist talk."

"Not being sexist. I just know what I like a woman's lips to do, and it has nothing to do with talking."

Heat filled her cheeks. She could only imagine what was on his mind. Yes, Pussy would like his women to do a whole load of other things rather than talk.

"How long have you been part of Chaos Bleeds?" she asked.

"Over ten years. I joined at a young age, and I've been a full member around the same length of time," he said.

"Do you have any family?"

"The club is my family."

She heard the scissors and felt the small tugs on the hair covering her pussy. Trying not to be embarrassed was the hardest thing she'd ever done.

"What made you settle down?" she asked.

"There's a club up in Fort Wills. They've stayed in the same place for a lifetime and only go on the road when the need requires. They're strong and happy. We're all getting older and moving from one state to another within a week has lost its appeal." He continued to work on her pubic hair as he spoke. She loved the way he talked. The deep rough tones of his voice made her melt. He had to see that she was turned on by what he was saying.

"Do you still ride?"

"Yes, I still ride. I've not got the need to change my location anymore. I've got nothing to hide."

She nodded. "I liked being on the back of your bike. It was fun."

"It's even better when you're not wearing a helmet."

"Maybe one day you'll let me ride without a helmet?" she asked, thinking about the wind in her face and what it would feel like to finally be free to enjoy life.

"Not a chance. You're wearing the helmet. I'm not risking your life for a little kick."

Sasha stayed silent as she listened to the snip of the scissors and felt the tugs lessen with every passing second.

"I bet watching the sun rise is the most amazing thing in the world. Growing up, I didn't pay it much attention. There always seemed more important stuff to deal with than watching the sun come up. Wish I had taken the time now to look."

He stopped, letting out a breath. "Actually, Sasha,

you're not missing anything. Yes, you can't see a sunrise or a sunset, but I can promise you that there's more important things to look forward to in life."

"Like what?"

Kenneth, when her mother wasn't around, would talk like he was reading off a list all the things she could no longer do or see. All the amazing beauty that was passing her by because she couldn't see anymore. Her stepfather was a fucking cruel bastard.

"Like this," he said.

Fingers slid through her slit. He touched her clit, and she cried out at the first contact.

"This is what you can feel. You don't need to see it to know how amazing it feels." He rubbed her clit, and she screamed as the pleasure crashed through her.

Chapter Six

Pussy saw the wonder on Sasha's face and knew in his heart he wanted to leave her feeling like that for years to come. She arched up against his touch, and he fingered her pussy. He'd trimmed away all of her excess pubic hair. All he needed to do was shave her.

"Are you still with me, baby?" he asked.

"Yes, I'm here."

She was breathless.

He moved his hand away from her clit. She let out a growl, and he chuckled. "Is my woman getting impatient?"

"You're not being fair."

"I'll be able to make you feel much better if you let me finish my work." He cleaned away the excess hair, finding the act incredibly intimate. Pussy washed a cloth and started to wet between her thighs. He took his time, enjoying the view before him.

Her eyes were closed as he went to work. Once he cleaned her, he opened up the fresh razor and placed the blade into place.

"I'm going to start to shave some of your hair. I've got some cream for you, but I need you to stay still," he said.

"I'm not going to go anywhere."

Staring up the length of her body, his cock answered to the call of her body. She was so beautiful that she made him ache to be inside her.

Take your time.

The longer he took preparing her and getting to know her the better it would be for him. He worked slowly, shaving away the hair that was in his way.

She didn't move as he worked, giving him plenty of time to work.

"Have you shaved a woman before?"

"No. I've seen a woman do it before." His thoughts drifted to Ashley, the best friend he'd lost. She'd died too soon.

"What are you thinking about?" she asked.

"Nothing."

"You've gone tense, and you're silent. Is it about the friend that you lost?"

He frowned. "How would you know that?"

"I've lost my dad, remember? It doesn't take a genius to know that you and your friend were involved."

Letting out a sigh, he swished the blade in the water before sliding the blade across the side of her pussy. He was almost done.

"I fucked Ashley often. We were best friends, but she didn't expect anything from me. I shared shit with her that I didn't with anyone else."

"Why didn't you marry her?" she asked.

Pussy chuckled. "If you knew Ashley, you would know she wasn't the marrying kind." Thinking about Ashley in white didn't sit well with him. She didn't want to get married. Ashley didn't trust in men. She trusted in the rules of the club and Devil. "She fucked all the club. Ashley wasn't a one man woman."

"Were you okay with that?"

"Yeah, I didn't want anything else from her. I'm not the jealous type." *However, when it comes to you, I refuse to share.*

There would be no way he'd leave her alone with other men from the club. None of the boys would take advantage of her, but Sasha was his woman.

"Really? You sound like a lot of women's ideal man."

He laughed. "I doubt that, baby. I'm not the jealous type, and I will not be told what I can and cannot do. I refuse to pick a woman to settle down with."

"It must be nice not having to worry about your life," she said.

Pussy frowned. He finished her pussy and wiped her clean. "How come you never got a dog?"

"What?"

"You know, the dogs that help blind people to get around."

Sasha's hands moved to her stomach. "Kenneth wouldn't get one for me. He spread a rumor around town that I was terrified of them."

"Don't you think it's strange he's trying to isolate you from everything you've ever known?" Pussy hated this man the more he found out.

"I'm blind. My mom adores him. I don't see a point in arguing with him. He's made of money, and I wasn't going to let my mom be unhappy."

"Yet, with him she's become a pill popping alcoholic?"

Running his fingers across the smooth lips of her sex, Pussy felt his cock harden. She was so fucking beautiful.

"You don't know her."

"You've got to be careful."

"I'm always careful."

He chuckled. "You're alone with me, Sasha. I wouldn't say you're careful." Getting to his feet, he stared down at her body. "I'm going to clean this away."

Pussy left her alone. In the bathroom, he cleaned away the mess he made and stared at his reflection in the cracked mirror.

What the fuck are you doing?

He was losing his mind. Sasha had dominated his thoughts from the first moment they met, and they'd not even seen each other. Staring at her in the diner, he thought she could see. Later on, when he found her left alone he'd found out the truth.

Don't mess with her.

Devil's words ran through his head. *"Don't fucking interrupt me. This girl, you've taken her away from her family and telling me you're not letting her back to the people who can protect her? Please, tell me, Pussy, if that's not laying fucking claim to her, what is?"*

He couldn't let her go back to that monster of a stepfather.

You're getting too involved.

Ashley appeared in his mind with her smiling face. They'd just fucked, and she'd given him an orgasm with her tits. She was lying on the bed with her feet kicked back in the air.

"What are you going to do if you ever fall in love?" Ashley asked.

"Simple, I'm never falling in love."

"You can't never fall in love. I bet the woman you finally give your heart to is going to be the most loved woman in the world. You're too sweet for your own good."

Pulling out of the memory, Pussy moved toward the doorway to watch Sasha. She was lying on the bed, tapping her foot in time to whatever tune was in her mind. He could never hurt her. She'd been hurt too much in her short life.

All he wanted to do was take her away from the pain and give her something to love. He knew he'd be good for her. She'd never want for anything.

Over the years he'd fucked many women and gotten what he wanted out of them. None of them left a lasting mark, not even Ashley. She only played in his mind because of their friendship. Sasha had taken him by surprise.

He'd take her to the clubhouse before he took her anywhere else.

Entering the bedroom, he cleared his throat.

"You're back?"

"Yes."

"You took a long time."

"I've been standing there watching you, baby. You've no idea how hot your body is." He gazed down at the bed and gave her a final chance to turn back. "This is your choice, Sasha. Once I get my jeans off, I'm going to fuck your tight cunt and make you feel on cloud nine." He heard her gasp. "This is your last chance to back out. I'll put my shirt on, help you get dressed and then we'll listen to a movie or something."

"I don't want to listen to a movie. I want you to fuck me, Pussy. I want you to show me how good it can be between a man and a woman."

"You know you'll get to feel this with a guy you deserve."

Why are you giving her a reason to stop tonight?

His cock was hard as a fucking rock, begging to get as close to her as possible.

"Do you not want to? If you don't want me then we can get dressed."

Before she finished, he removed his jeans, kicking his boots across the room. He wanted her. Kneeling on the bed, he took hold of her hand and placed her fingers around his shaft. "Baby, wanting you is not a problem. I fucking ache for you."

She squeezed his cock. A V formed between her eyebrows. "Why do you keep asking me if I want to stop?"

"I don't want you to wake up in the morning and regret giving your cherry to a fucking asshole. I'm not the kind of man you deserve."

Her smile lit up her whole face, and Pussy felt himself falling. He'd seen women in the Chaos Bleeds and The Skulls MC sporting that same kind of expression. Lexie looked at Devil as if he could walk on water.

"You're sweet. My sweet, bad-ass biker." She moved her hand up and down his shaft, peeling back the skin. He groaned. "What's the matter? Did I hurt you?"

She withdrew her hand.

"Everything you do is fine." He leaned down and brushed his lips against hers. "I'm going to need you to talk to me, tell me what you like."

"I will."

Stroking a finger down her face, he caressed over her breast. She was ripe for the plucking.

You're going to be the first man in her life and the last.

Pussy stared down into her unseeing eyes and knew he wasn't going to be able to let her go after this night. The last few months he'd been trying to catch the merest glimpse of her. He drove through town trying to avoid the places he'd seen her. His brothers would be at the diner, and he'd try not to look for her or stare at her when he did see her.

She'd become his hidden obsession.

Moving between her spread thighs, he glanced down at her shaved pussy. "I'm going to lick and kiss every inch of your body." He claimed her lips before she had a chance to comment. Caressing down her body, he fingered her breasts, sliding his hands down to cup her cunt. He slipped a finger through her wet slit, feeling her wetness soak his finger.

Kissing down her neck, he licked over her pulse and flicked the tips of her nipples with his tongue.

"Pussy?"

"Yes, baby." He muttered the response against her body, loving the sound of his name on her lips.

"What … are … you … doing?" Each word came out on a gasp.

Dipping his tongue down into her belly button, he felt her body shake from the smallest of touches.

"I'm getting to know your body," he said. He slipped between her open thighs and stared at her pussy. "I've done an excellent job with your cunt."

****

Sasha cried out as he opened the lips of her sex. Fisting the blanket, she tried to bring focus to her crazy, blank world. Everything he did seemed highlighted by touch. There was nothing more for her to do other than hold on as he took her for a ride.

"So fucking pretty."

Something wet, she guessed his tongue, slid through her slit. As quickly as he started, he pulled away. "This here." He pressed his thumb against her. Pleasure took over her body. Arching up, she tried to thrust against his thumb as well as get away from him. "That's your clit, and I'm going to flick my tongue over you until you come all over my mouth. I want to swallow your cum."

"You weren't lying about talking."

"No, I wasn't. I need you to tell me what you're feeling, even if you moan out. Don't keep any of those precious sounds away from me."

"I won't." She wouldn't dare deny him.

Everything he'd done to her body had been to give her pleasure.

She heard more movement, and then his tongue flicked her clit.

Crying out, she jerked on the bed. One of his hands pressed on her stomach. She covered his hand with her own trying to stop him from holding her down. Nothing stopped him from doing what he wanted to do. He held her down easily and ravished her pussy. His tongue flicked, stroked, and lapped up her juices.

Fighting the pleasure was useless. Pussy was in control. All she could do was trust him as he took her down this path.

"Pussy?"

"I know, baby. Relax, let go, and I'll be here to catch you. I won't let anything happen to you."

She trusted him more than she trusted her own mother.

The pleasure built inside her. Letting out a gasp, she fisted her hands in the blankets and screamed as her release crashed into her. She thrashed on the bed, and Pussy held her down, stroking her clit.

"It's too much," she said.

"Let it take over. I've got you."

Her release went on and on. Throughout it all, Pussy held her, comforted her. He continued to touch her, whisper endearments to her as she came down.

"There, baby," he said, kissing her lips. She tasted her cream on his lips.

She ran her tongue over his lips.

"Do you like the taste of yourself?" he asked.

The taste didn't offend her, and she shrugged. "Thank you."

"Thank you for letting me taste your sweetness." He slid his tongue into her mouth, and she opened her lips wider for him.

"Are you going to fuck me now?"

Sasha didn't want him to forget or get turned off by her.

"I'll grab the condom."

"I wish I could see so I knew what you looked

like."

"I'm an ugly ass, baby. Believe me when I tell you that you're a sucker for a talented tongue," he said.

She chuckled. His good humor was one of the elements she loved about him.

Don't say love. He doesn't do love. She wouldn't risk him not coming around anymore.

"I bet you're hot," she said.

"You've not been around enough men to know that." The bed dipped again. "I've got the condom on. I'm not going to lie to you. This could hurt. I'll go slow." He rested between her thighs, and she hated not being able to see him. Reaching out, she touched his arms, and he pressed his body to her.

"I hate this," she said.

"Baby." He cupped her cheek. The tenderness of his touch wasn't lost on her. "You not being able to see doesn't bother me. Being able to see your face and knowing I've put that wonder and the smile on it means the world to me." His lips grazed hers.

He jerked, and she felt the tip of his cock press against her.

She gasped, and he slid his tongue into her mouth.

"There's only you," he said, slamming deep inside her.

Screaming at the explosion of pain, she gripped his arms as he held her hips. He didn't move, but his head pressed to her forehead, holding her down.

"I've got you, Sasha. I'm not letting you go."

"It hurts."

"I know it hurts, but it'll be over in a moment. Stay with me, talk to me."

"It's dark." She moaned, wishing for once she was able to see his face.

"I've got messy blond hair, baby. There was a time when I shaved it all off, but I like my hair. It's too hard to be bald."

She chuckled and winced as the pain struck her again.

"I've got brown eyes. They're a lighter color than yours, and my body is covered in ink. I don't work out for fun. I do it to pass the time, and to be part of the club I need to be strong. They all depend on me."

Both of his hands moved to her face.

"I'm sorry for hurting you."

"You don't need to be sorry." She tried to smile.

"And you don't need to wish to be able to see. I can see for the both of us, and I know I'm the lucky guy here."

Gripping his arms, Sasha was charmed by his words.

"You know what to say to make me fall for you."

He didn't tense or say anything.

Moments passed, and he took the time to kiss her lips. "I'm going to start moving now. Tell me if it hurts too much."

Pussy eased out of her. She tensed up expecting to feel nothing but pain. There was no pain as he moved out of her. When only the tip of him remained inside her, she whimpered.

"Please, don't stop," she said. He pressed inside going deep within her.

The pain changed, turning into something amazing. She didn't know what it was only that she wanted that feeling to never end.

"Tell me what you're feeling, Sasha?"

"It feels wonderful, Pussy. Please don't stop."

"Call me Shane."

She spoke his name, and he thrust back inside

her.

"That's it. When we're here, alone and my dick's inside you, call me Shane."

Groaning, she met him thrust for thrust. He kissed her deeply, and she followed him and his movements.

"It has never been like this before," he said.

He sounded amazed.

Pussy moved one of his arms behind her head, and holding onto the back of her neck with his other hand, he cupped her hip. They were body to body. His chest to her breasts, every inch of them was touching.

He surrounded her with warmth. His cock was like a brand inside her pussy. She knew there was never going to be another man for her. Pussy had shattered all of her expectations with his words and body. He took her on a ride that was more than just sex to her. She was too far involved already.

His hand went from her hip to grip her hand. Pussy slammed in deep, over and over again. She felt his cock push through the muscles of her pussy. Clenching down on him, she lost all of her senses as pleasure took over.

"What have you done to me?" he asked.

She didn't respond. He didn't need to hear her talking. His lips wrought havoc with her mind as he kissed her. She'd fallen for Pussy, and it wasn't just down to this one chance fuck. No, he'd ruined her the moment he stopped to talk to her months ago. His voice played over her mind all the time.

"So fucking good," he said, plunging inside her.

Holding onto his body, she cried out as another orgasm took her unawares.

Pussy followed her into bliss, groaning out his release. His cock jerked inside her, and he collapsed on top of her. He was heavy, but she loved the feel of him against her. The darkness no longer felt so scary with Pussy in her life. He'd given her so much in such a short time.

"That was amazing," he said, kissing her head.

Don't keep it to yourself.

"Don't freak out, okay," she said.

"What is it? Did I hurt you?"

"I think I'm in love with you. I know it means nothing to you, and this was just a one-time thing. I need you know how I feel."

He tensed but didn't pull away from her.

"I don't do love."

"I do."

"How can you know you love me?" he asked.

She forced the tears back that wanted to fall. "I just do. I feel it inside."

He jerked away from her. "I'm going to go and clean up."

You've fucked up.

Air met her body. She frowned. "I don't expect anything from you. I'm not waiting for a confession of love. I knew you couldn't love me, Shane."

She started to panic. Getting to her feet, she tripped up, landing in a heap on the floor.

"Fuck," he said, cursing.

Sasha tried to reach out to get to her feet. Air met her arms again. Growling in frustration, she had no choice but to accept his help on the bed.

"You don't have to help me."

"Yeah, I do."

With her ass on the bed, she pushed him away. "I don't need your help."

"Look, I'm sorry for being a dick."

"You can take me back home."

"I'm not taking you back to that dick." She heard

him sigh. "Shit, I'm sorry. I shouldn't have reacted like that. I don't know what you want from me."

"I don't want anything. I told you not to freak out on me. I'm not asking for anything."

"I'm not used to being like this."

"Don't worry, I won't tell you anything like that again." She folded her arms over her breasts.

"You're not going back home. You're staying with me, and I'm going to clean you up."

She squealed as he picked her up and carried her through to the bathroom. "You can't do this to me."

"Actually, I can, and there's nothing you can do to stop me." He placed her down on her feet, keeping her steady with a hand under her elbow. "We're going to take a long wash, and then we're going to deal with everything else.

Sasha nodded. "Fine."

Her body was starting to ache, and even though he'd pissed her off, she didn't want to leave him.

What did that say about her?

She didn't know and chose not to think about it.

****

"They've fucking taken her, and now Penny is freaking out," Kenneth said, pacing his office. Frederick sat behind the desk as if he had every right to be there with his fingers touching in front of him. The action reminded Kenneth of a cartoon evil villain, contemplating his next move.

"And you're sure Chaos Bleeds has something to do with this?"

"Yes. Everyone I spoke to told me she'd gone with one of the men." He couldn't control her if she believed she could do shit on her own. Not only couldn't he control her, but he also couldn't make sure she found some freak accident that finally put her in the ground.

Kenneth was so fucking angry. How dare one of those evil fuckers think they could ruin his future?

He needed more money before he finally went into retirement. He'd fallen for Sasha's mother, Penny, the first moment he saw her. Finding out she had a daughter had annoyed him, but he also knew there was no way of getting rid of Sasha yet. When they started arguing and he'd thrown her downstairs, he'd been panicked. The last thing he wanted to do was be sent to prison for murder. If Sasha was to meet with an "accident" that took her life then he didn't have to worry about it. Frederick could fix that and take care of her irritating mother.

"The Chaos Bleeds crew is doing me favors, Kenneth. I can't stop them from taking what they want."

"I do you more favors. You practically own this town because of what I did." Running fingers through his hair, Kenneth was so fucking angry. All of his careful planning was about to be smashed to smithereens. Sasha's blindness had been a problem, distracting Penny. In the beginning he had seen Sasha as someone to control. Then that got tiresome, and now he just wanted Sasha out of the picture altogether with no way of it coming back on him. He wanted Penny all to himself

"I'm grateful to you for your favors, but I want to remind you, Kenneth, I can fucking squash you like the bug you are. Now, I will ask Devil to give me back the girl and you can take her from me, but I can't promise you they won't come back and get her themselves," he said.

"I don't care what you have to do. Get me back Sasha for Penny. I need her to die at the right time, when Penny has only me for support."

He'd take all of the crew out if he could. All he wanted was Penny's daughter so that he could continue with his plan. Over the years he'd put in a lot of time with Penny and Sasha. He wasn't going to let anything happen to Penny or let the shitty biker crew spoil his future. Penny still loved her daughter. All he needed to do was push the right buttons, and Penny would be eating out of the palm of his hand in no time when her daughter was dead. She was eating out of it now to a point, but Sasha stayed between them. He'd have killed Sasha a long time ago if he could have gotten away with it, but it wouldn't do him any good if Penny blamed him for Sasha's death.

Chapter Seven

In the middle of the night, Pussy stared down into Sasha's sleeping face. She was too sweet and trusting for her own good. He tucked behind her ear some hair that was obstructing his view. After he'd showered her, removing the evidence of her virgin blood, he'd tucked her in bed. Lying next to her, he'd fallen asleep, but he was awake again.

She loves me.

He didn't deserve her love. She should be with a man who'd give her everything her heart desired. Four years she'd been screwed over by that bastard, and he wouldn't even let her have a dog to help her. Everything Kenneth did to her made Pussy uneasy. Her stepfather had to be isolating her on purpose. There was no other explanation for what he was doing. Her mother was hooked on pills and booze whereas Sasha was beautiful. She rivaled Angel's sweetness as far as he was concerned.

You can't let her go.

No, he couldn't let her go, and he didn't want to think why.

"What am I going to do with you?" he asked, speaking the words aloud.

Sasha continued to sleep on.

You can't leave her. Claim her for your own.

"Shane?" Her eyes opened, and she frowned. Taking hold of her hand, he placed her palm against his chest.

"I'm here, baby."

"You're awake? Is it morning?"

"No. I couldn't sleep."

She closed her eyes again. "What are you doing?" she asked.

"I'm watching you, and I was thinking about something."

Reaching behind him, he took another condom.

Don't wear it.

He hesitated. Would it be wrong to fuck her without a condom? If she was pregnant with his child then he could use that excuse to claim her as his old lady.

Don't do it. She deserves better than that.

Tearing into the foil, he rolled the rubber over his cock.

"What were you thinking about?" she asked.

Sliding between her thighs, he ran a finger through her creamy slit. She'd be sore, but he had no intention of rushing this time. Pressing the tip of his cock to her entrance, he stared down into her face and slowly glided inside her. He didn't want to hurt her.

She groaned, arching up to him.

"You becoming my old lady." He gripped her around the back and lifted up. Pussy turned so his back was to the headboard and Sasha's legs were wrapped around his waist with his cock buried deep inside her.

Sasha gasped. Her nails sank into the flesh of his shoulders.

"What does that mean?"

"You become mine. I claim you and marry you."

He gripped her hips, pulling her off his cock until only the tip remained inside her. Pussy growled as her pussy tightened around his shaft while bringing her back down. He thrust inside her a couple more times before he kept her steady.

"Is that a proposal?"

"Yes, I guess it was." He'd never win awards for romance. Fortunately, he wasn't looking to win any kind of awards at the moment.

"You don't love me."

"I don't need to love you to want to take care of you. Your stepfather has an ulterior motive when it comes to you, baby. I don't want to see you hurt." He pushed some hair off the back of her neck. Placing his palm over her pulse, he felt how erratically it was beating.

"But you don't love me?"

"No, I don't."

"Do you know how crazy this sounds? My stepfather hasn't got anything planned. He's happy making his deals and treating my mother like shit. There's nothing going on." She didn't try to push him away.

"You're blind, without any means of fending for yourself. Do you think it's a coincidence your mother is addicted to pills and booze? She's got to have been given a reason for going for them. You said she wasn't always like this. How do you know he hasn't encouraged her to become this?" Pussy asked. No matter what she said, he wasn't letting her go back to Kenneth. He was sure the Italian guy was Frederick. If so, then Frederick had a lot more plans than running shit and using them as some kind of delivery service.

"My mom's strong."

"She lost your father, and Kenneth turned up out of the blue when she wasn't at her best. He took her, molded her into what he wanted."

Sasha rested her head against his chest. "What do you want me to do?" she asked.

"I want you to become my old lady. Marry me, Sasha and I can protect you. The club can protect you once you're mine." The lies poured out of his mouth. The moment he took her to the club, they'd protect her. She was a woman in need, and they'd all do everything in their power to protect her.

"Will you help my mom? Take her away from him for good?" she asked.

"Is that the deal breaker?"

"Yes. You've got to promise to take care of my mom, or I won't do anything you say."

He knew he could force her hand. "I'll do it."

Taking her chin in his hands, he stared into her face. She couldn't see him. Her eyes were staring at his chin. It didn't bother him.

You're falling for her.

Taking a deep breath, he returned his grip to her hips. Easing out of her tight cunt, he slammed in deep. She cried out, gripping his shoulders with a death grip that surprised him.

Over and over he slammed inside her, never letting up.

She circled her arms around his neck.

You took her virginity, her heart, and now you're ruining any chance of another man giving her what you can.

He cut the thoughts off, no longer caring what he was doing.

Watching her face as she reached orgasm and feeling her pussy tighten was more than enough for him right now. Everything else could make sense in time. The only sense he needed to make of his actions was getting her to trust him.

"Fuck me, Sasha." She took over, rolling her hips, taking him deep inside.

Her eyes closed as she arched up against him. He gazed at her tits as they bounced with each thrust.

As he cupped her cheek, the beginnings of his orgasm started up. He didn't avert his gaze as she rode him into an earth shattering climax. This time she collapsed over him. Sliding down on the bed, she moved her legs out of the way. When she made to pull away from him, he wouldn't let her move. He held her tightly against him.

"Pussy?"

"I don't want to move. I want to hold onto you. There's no need for us to move yet." Stroking her hair, he closed his own eyes, inhaling her scent.

I don't want to leave this moment.

She was breaking apart his entire world. Pussy didn't want to let her go. Letting her go would risk ruining himself. No other woman would ever touch a part of him like she did.

"I love you, Shane."

The words were on the tip of his tongue, but he kept them at bay. She wouldn't believe him now.

"What happens now?" she asked.

"I take you to the clubhouse. We're going to need to talk with Devil about getting married, and then we'll deal with your mom."

"Please, don't let her get hurt because of this." She looked up at him, resting her chin on her hand. For a split second her gaze was on his. He was sure she could see him.

She couldn't; he knew that.

Her fingers ran over his skin. Did she have any idea what her touch was doing to his body? Pussy couldn't focus with her touch.

"We won't let anything happen to her."

Sasha lay back down, and he hoped she didn't notice the tension inside him.

"Shane?"

"Yeah."

"This is just between us, right?" she asked.

Frowning, he stopped touching her back. "What do you mean?"

"There won't be any other women or men. This is us now, right?"

"I don't share, Sasha. You agree to be mine, and you wear my ring, then no one else. I'll be the only man you come to when you need me."

She licked her lips. "Then I want the same."

"Huh?"

"No other women. Not even best friend sex. You want sex, then come to me. I know there are better women out there with more experience, but I want you to come to me."

There's no one else I want.

"Baby, you're the only woman I'm interested in. You've got no chance of me going anywhere else."

She dropped her head back down, and within minutes she was fast asleep. He listened to the sweet sounds she made as she drifted off.

You've got to take care of her now. She's going to depend on you.

"I love you, Sasha." He whispered the words when he was sure she was fast asleep. He didn't know why he waited, only that he did.

****

"You've got to be fucking kidding me," Devil said, the following afternoon. Sasha sat in a chair. She didn't know if she was in the main part of the club or an office. From how loud Devil shouted, she was starting to think it was an office. He hurt her head by shouting that loud. Pussy stood behind her chair with his hands on her shoulders.

His presence helped to calm her nerves. She was sure there were more people than Devil, Pussy, and herself.

Sasha made sure to call him Pussy rather than Shane. They were not in the bedroom anymore. This morning he'd woken her up a second time to make love to her. She loved the way he claimed her. The sex was amazing. She didn't know for sure if they'd fucked, made love, or had sex. There seemed to be multiple ways of doing it.

Great, she was starting to sound like a young girl in her own mind. Pussy wouldn't want a young girl. He needed a woman by his side, and from the way his boss was shouting, he needed her now.

"I told you I wasn't letting her back there," Pussy said.

"Devil, you need to listen to him."

"Lex, stay the fuck out of this. I'm sick and tired of my fucking men thinking they can do whatever shit they want."

She didn't recognize the female's voice. However, she was never going to forget Devil. Sasha never wanted to meet him down a dark alley.

Silence met his outburst.

"Oh, boss, you're so not getting laid tonight," Pussy said. She loved the way he teased. His voice changed, became lighter somehow.

"Shut the fuck up," Devil said.

"Why should he shut up? He's right. You're so not getting near me tonight."

The noise of someone walking away met her ears. She tensed in her seat.

"Shit, Lex, I'm sorry."

"No, you're not. I don't give a fuck what this Gonzalez guy is doing. You're better than him, and yet you're behaving like this." Lex let out a growl. "He's got you and Tiny torn apart. Stop behaving like children in a playground and start seeing this as men. I'm not raising two kids on my own."

A door slammed, and Sasha tensed.

"It's okay, baby. Boss lady just left, and boss man is so not getting any sex tonight."

"I mean it, Pussy. Don't fucking push me on this."

More noise and she imagined Devil had sat down.

"What's going on?" Pussy asked.

"I can't tell you in front of her."

"She's the reason we're here, Devil. Look, if you don't want me to make a claim on her then tell me," Pussy said. He stayed behind her giving her shoulders a little squeeze.

"Would you still stay in the club?" Devil asked.

"No, I'd leave. She can't go back to that monster. I won't allow it."

"Can I speak plainly?" Devil asked.

"Yeah."

"No, I'm not talking to you. I'm talking to her."

The conversation went on around her. Frustration gnawed at her. "What?" she asked.

"You're blind, love. You're a liability. It sounds to me your stepfather has big plans for you as well as your mother, and I've not met the bastard." She shuddered at the thought. "You could get us all killed. You can't have our backs or help us fight."

"Devil?"

"No, Pussy. Judi can shoot, Lex can fight, and Mia can certainly take care of herself. No one has a chance against Phoebe. She'd kill you in a heartbeat if threatened. Your woman, she can't do anything."

Sasha tensed. There *was* nothing she could do.

"She's mine, Devil. I don't give a fuck what she can do. You know as well as I do that you'd avoid Lex hurting anyone. Ripper would tear anyone apart for hurting Judi, and Curse would make sure Mia was always protected." Pussy's anger was starting to show through. The teasing was long gone.

"You're asking us to protect a woman who cannot take care of herself."

A chair scraped along the floor. She squeezed her legs together, trapping her hands between her thighs. The sudden sounds terrified her.

Don't be scared. There's nothing to be scared of.

"Pussy, stand down," another male said.

"No. I've been part of this fucking club for over ten fucking years. You're telling me that my choice of woman isn't good enough?" Pussy asked, growling out the words.

"Pussy?"

His hands left her shoulders.

"I'll put my fucking jacket down now and leave this shit behind."

"You'd turn your back on the club for this woman?" Devil asked.

Was a fight about to break out around her? She didn't know what to do and stayed sat in her chair. It would be best if she kept to herself.

"Pussy, don't do this." The mystery man spoke up again.

"Yes, I'd leave, and I wouldn't come fucking back. You and Tiny are welcome to the mess you're getting yourselves into," Pussy said. "I'll turn my back and make it with her."

He'd do that for her, and yet he didn't love her? It made no sense. No man would turn his back on the world he loved for a woman he didn't care about.

"I wasn't always blind," she said, hoping to avoid conflict. There's no way she'd come out of this fight unscathed. She couldn't avoid punches when she didn't know the way they were coming.

"I know, baby. He knows this."

"I'm not asking you to leave the club, Pussy," Devil said.

"Then what the fuck are you asking?" Pussy spat the words out. She winced, thankful his wrath was not directed at her.

"She's going to need your protection. Think about what you're doing before you do."

"I've had months to think about that. I'm not making a mistake here, Devil. Arrange the fucking priest. I'm marrying Sasha, and I don't give a fuck how much I have to protect her."

Silence met his answer. She jumped as he gripped her elbow.

"Fine, you want to take that challenge, then we'll stick by your side."

"You don't have to do this," she said.

"I'm doing this. We're going to get married."

"We've got a lot more to discuss, Pussy. Take her to Lex and the women. We've got a meeting to get through first."

She was lifted out of the chair, and they started walking. Pussy wrapped an arm around her waist, leading her away.

"That was tense, and I couldn't even see him." She tried to make light of what happened.

"He shouldn't worry, and neither should you."

"The man has a point. I'm not exactly a viable partner for you," she said.

Pussy stopped. His hands cupped her face. "You're the only one I want. I don't care what I've got to do. I'm going to protect you, Sasha."

"I'm not Ashley," she said.

"I know. You're the woman I want." He dropped a kiss to her lips. "Come on, I'll introduce you to the other women. They're the old ladies, so they'll treat you with respect."

He opened doors for her, being patient as she walked through them.

"I tell you, he talks to me like that again and he can suck his own cock," Lexie said.

Sasha recognized the woman's voice and couldn't help but smile at what she said.

"You do that, Lex. You get him to suck his own cock and film it. It'll be awesome for us little people to see," Pussy said, his teasing back in place.

"Shut up, Pussy. You're going to give him a heart attack with the way you're acting," she said. "Hey, I'm Lexie."

Lexie touched her arm. Pushing her hand out, Sasha gingerly shook the other woman's hand. "I'm Sasha. It's nice to meet you."

"Will you take care of her while we're in a meeting?" Pussy said.

"Sure thing. I won't cause any problems if I was you," Lexie said.

"I never cause any problems." The hand on her shoulder tightened. "I'll be back in no time, babe. Lex will take care of you. She takes care of everyone."

He kissed her temple then left the room. Letting out a breath, she noticed Lexie hadn't released her hand.

"Come on, sweetie. We're not going to bite or hurt you." She tugged on her hand, and Sasha followed her. "Here, there's a seat."

Perching on the seat, she tried to think of who was in the room.

"I'm Phoebe, honey. I'm married to Vincent. He runs the strip club in town."

Sasha nodded, noticing her slightly deeper voice.

"It's nice to meet you," she said.

Running her hands down her thighs, she

wondered what they thought of her.

"I'm Judi." A woman touched her palm. "It's nice to see Pussy fighting for someone again. Ever since Ashley died, he's been a little dead inside."

A sob filled the room.

"That's Mia. She was best friends with Ashley," Judi said.

"I'm sorry. Her death is still raw," Mia said. "I'm with Curse. So, you're Pussy's woman."

"Yes. I mean, I think I'm his woman. He won't let me return to my parents' house or at least my mother. It's a little messed up." She stopped speaking.

"You can talk all you want here, honey. We're not going to hold it against you. When I'm alone with Devil tonight I'm going to crush his balls for the way he talked to me," Lexie said.

Sasha chuckled. "He didn't sound very nice."

"He's a wonderful man. Shit's happening right now that he can't control, and it pisses him off."

"I know what that's like."

The women murmured their agreement. Feeling like they understood her, Sasha started to relax. They wouldn't hurt her. She was safe in the clubhouse with these women.

"Besides, I can't hurt him too much. I love sex as much as he does. I'd ruin any chance of getting any myself," Lexie said.

Sasha burst out laughing, loving the woman more. Her voice sounded calm and soothing.

"You evil little shits. Give me back my daughter."

Frowning, Sasha jerked at the sound. It was Kenneth.

The sound of glass shattering and a groan followed.

"What the fuck?" Phoebe said. "Lexie?"

She couldn't see or do anything.

"No, I'm fine," Lexie said, disoriented.

"You've just been hit in the head with a brick," Judi said. "Sit still."

Doors opened, and Sasha got to her feet, hoping there was something she could do. What could she do? Devil was right. She couldn't even help Lexie.

Chapter Eight

"We've got another shipment of girls to transport to Fort Wills," Devil said, the instant the door was closed. Pussy fisted his palm. Every time they sat down to a meeting it was about Frederick Gonzalez. The Italian criminal who had his fingers in so many pies, making their lives shit. Though at first he'd mentioned his respect for The Skulls, now, Frederick owned the other biker club as well as Chaos Bleeds.

"We're not our own club anymore," Death said. "All we are is a fucking delivery service. Instead of delivering pizza and takeout, we serve pussy to the nation and whatever drug is making the rounds."

"Our job is becoming too risky. It will only be a matter of time before the Feds get involved. You'll be seeing Lexie and the kids through a cell, Devil. Something has to give soon," Ripper said. "The risks are too great."

Devil rubbed a hand down his face. "Life would be so much easier if we could put a bullet in his head."

"We can at the right time, in the right moment. Butch beat the shit out of him. What's to say we can't push back?" Curse said.

Pussy listened to all of their suggestions.

"Remember what he did as payback," Snake said. "The entire compound was raided and he got their kids took off them. We've got to be smart about this. We can't rush into anything."

"I know," Devil said.

"These girls have got to be the last. I'm sure we delivered a fucking adolescent last time. Shit." Devil grabbed the paperweight from his desk and launched it across the room.

"We need to work with The Skulls," Vincent

said. "This is not something we can do alone. Frederick has cops, Feds, and I bet even more men on hand to do his work. We do this slowly, and we make sure we're the ones in control. I'm not risking seeing Phoebe and my boys from a cell. It's not going to happen, and I'm not spending time in prison with men wanting to make me their bitch."

Pussy couldn't argue with the man. "I'm with Vincent. There's got to be a time and place to do this shit."

The sound of crashing filled the air. Phoebe's shout of Lexie's name had Devil charging out the door. All of them followed their president. One of the windows in the main room was smashed. Glancing down at Lexie, Pussy saw blood spilling down the side of her head. She looked dazed as Phoebe tried to help her up.

Sasha stood looking frustrated and sick. Going to her side, he touched her cheek. She jerked back. "It's me, baby. What's going on?"

"I don't know. Is Lexie okay? I think she was hurt with a brick, but I can't be sure."

"She's fine." He didn't give Lexie a thought as he looked at how shaken up his own woman was.

"Are you sure? I heard Phoebe talk about a brick."

"I'm fine, Devil. Who was the fucker who threw it?" Lexie said.

"Give me back my fucking daughter now, you sick fucks."

Pussy recognized that voice. Turning toward the sound of yelling, he saw Kenneth in the parking lot.

"That fucker threw a brick at my woman." Devil handed his woman to Phoebe.

"Stay with them. I'll be back in a moment," Pussy said.

"Don't let him hurt you," Sasha called after him.

He wasn't going to let anyone hurt him. Pussy was going to hurt this fucker and enjoy it while it happened.

Devil slammed open the front door to the clubhouse. The sweet-butts were nowhere in sight.

"Who the fuck are you?" Devil asked, shouting the words. He was removing his jacket as he walked.

"Me? I'm the guy who can shut you the fuck down. I want Sasha, and I want her now. I know you filthy fuckers have her." Kenneth no longer looked like a respectable man. He looked like the evil fucker he was.

An expensive looking car was parked outside the gate. A pretty looking woman was swigging from a bottle of vodka as she looked at Kenneth. She had to be Sasha's mother. The woman looked scared stiff of this man, but Pussy saw how pretty she was. Both women had been trapped because of Kenneth.

"You think throwing bricks at my fucking clubhouse, at my fucking wife, is going to get you what you want?" Devil asked.

Pussy was waiting for any reason to take this fucker out. He was tired of being ordered around and fucked over. This man had hurt Sasha. He'd blinded her, used her, and now it was time for him to pay the price.

"I don't give a fuck. Give me back my daughter now," Kenneth said.

"Your daughter is unharmed, but my wife isn't." Devil stepped right up to the man. He was a good foot taller than Kenneth and wider.

Pussy saw a flash of fear in Kenneth's eyes, but he didn't back down.

"Give me back my daughter."

"I want an apology for my wife." Devil spat the words at the other man. "Now."

"I'm not apologizing to your wife."

The moment was interrupted as another car pulled up outside of the clubhouse. Pussy saw Frederick Gonzalez get out of the back along with Ronald and Homer, his two cronies. One of them had killed Ashley. In his mind, he saw her severed head.

"Devil, I'd back down if I was you."

Frederick approached, buttoning up his jacket. He gave off the air of being in control.

These fuckers are going to die.

"He hurt my woman."

"She's not dead, is she?" Frederick asked. Devil gritted his teeth but remained silent. "Excellent. Then you don't touch Kenneth. He's a friend of mine, and I don't let my friends get hurt."

"Ashley was your friend," Pussy said, tensing ready to fight.

"No, Ashley was a woman given to me to fuck. She passed her sell by date."

"You fucker," Mia said, yelling. None of them had seen the women come out. Mia rushed past them all before they had time to react. She landed a blow to Frederick's chest. Curse tugged her off. "You evil fucking bastard. She didn't deserve to die. Ashley was a sweet woman. You're a fucking monster who deserves to die." She fought Curse to try to get to Gonzalez. Her sobs could be heard throughout the clubhouse.

What were they doing working for this fucker?

"I'll take care of it," Curse said. He was whispering to his woman over and over. Lexie joined her man, glaring at Kenneth.

"I'm fine, baby," she said.

Blood was dripping from a cut on the side of her head, an instant bruise forming.

"I suggest you keep your women in check, Devil.

They're getting a little too feisty for my liking."
Frederick ran a hand down his creased suit. "I didn't kill
her. I've got people to do it."

Pussy saw the smirk on Homer's face. He tensed
up and charged at the other man. Tackling him to the
ground, he slammed Homer's head against the tarmac.
"You fucking killed her?"

He didn't give Homer chance to say anything as
he perched over him, landing blow after blow against the
man.

Devil grabbed his arm and tugged him off the
man. "Back away."

"He killed fucking Ashley." He needed to avenge
his friend. Ashley had been his best friend. He saw her
smiling in his mind. They'd taken that away from her,
and Pussy was never going to get that back.

"Sasha is out in the open. I need you to hold your
shit together," Devil said.

"I'll hold my shit together as long as I can.
You've got to promise me, we're going to take these
fuckers out."

Devil nodded.

Stepping back, he joined the rest of his brothers
in staring at Frederick.

"Now, I'm just disappointed," Frederick said.
"We're all friends, and yet you're attacking my friends."

"You killed one of ours. You owe us," Mia said,
speaking up.

No one stopped her. She was right in what she
said.

Glancing behind him, he saw Sasha standing
alone. Reaching out, he grasped her hand and tugged her
closer to him. She didn't fight him.

"Sasha," Kenneth said.

She tensed in Pussy's arms. There was no chance

of him letting her go back to that evil fucker. It wasn't happening. He watched with satisfaction as Homer had to be helped up onto his feet. At least he'd gotten in some good punches before it was taken away from him.

"You don't get to talk to her."

"Sasha, honey," her mother said.

Her mother had climbed out of the car and come to join them. Pussy noticed the anger in Kenneth's face. Yeah, he couldn't let either woman go back with this fucker. There were plans brewing inside him, and Pussy knew they weren't good plans.

"Mom, what are you doing here?" Sasha wrapped her arms around his body, holding onto him.

"You need to come home, sweetie. Your father and I are very worried."

Sasha shook her head. "No, I'm here with Pussy. He's asked me to marry him, and I've said yes."

That's right, fucker, she's mine.

"No, I don't accept this. He's coerced her into accepting," Kenneth said. "She can't get married without our permission."

"I'm over eighteen, and you're not my father. My father died a long time ago, and he'd be happy with my decision." She snuggled in against him. "I don't want to leave."

"You're not going anywhere." Pussy kissed the top her head. "Tell your mother you want her here with you." He whispered the words so no one else would hear. "You've got to trust me. He's going to hurt her otherwise and use her to get what he wants."

"Mom, will you stay with me tonight? Please, I'd like for us to catch up and have some girly fun."

He watched her mother sigh. "Of course, honey. I'll stay." She crossed from their side onto his. Her mother was protected now. Glaring at Kenneth, Pussy made sure the other man knew who had won this time.

"You can't do this, Penny. You don't need to stay with her."

"She's my daughter, Kenneth. I'll talk to you later, and I'm going to make sure she's okay," Penny said.

"I'm afraid, Kenneth, you're going to have to deal with her decision. I'm sure she'll come to her senses soon enough," Frederick said. "As always, Devil, it was a pleasure doing business with you."

"Not so fucking fast," Devil said.

Pussy watched as Devil swung back and slammed his fist against Kenneth's face hard, knocking the uptight asshole on his butt. "That's for hurting my wife. I suggest you afford a guard. When I see you next, I'm going to fucking kill you." Devil picked up Lexie and walked back into the building.

Pussy looked at Homer, remembering every part of his body. The next time they met, Pussy was the only one coming out alive.

****

"Honey, what the hell is going on? Finding out you were missing scared me. I begged Kenneth to not stop looking until he found you. It's not like you to not come home. When he found out about you, he wouldn't stop ranting about the biker group in town. I couldn't get him to make any sense," her mother said.

"I'm sorry, Mom. I shouldn't have left you in the dark like that." She was sitting on Pussy's bed while her mother bustled around the room, clearly tidying up the mess. "Mom, sit with me. This is his room, and he'll like it done a certain way."

"It's filthy."

"It's his room." Sasha waited until the bed dipped.

Her mother took hold of her hands, running shaking fingers over her wrist. She was going into withdrawal already, and it had been at least two hours since she last drank. Sasha was worried.

"Mom, you've got a problem."

"I know I have, honey. Don't you think I don't know that?" She heard her mother sob. "When did things start to get so fucking bad? When did I mess up?"

"Mom?" She reached up and placed a hand on her cheek. "It's not your fault."

"Yes, it is. I'm the one who brought him into our home. I let him near you. If I'd been sensible you wouldn't be sitting here blind." She listened as her mother withdrew and started to sob. "It's all my fault. I shouldn't have taken the pills and started drinking. You needed me most, and I chose to look the other way. What kind of a parent am I if I can't even look after my own daughter? When he told me you fell downstairs, I didn't think it was possible, but I believed him."

Sasha wished there was something she could say to make it all better for her. There was nothing. Kenneth entered their lives, built up some fantasy world for her mother, and then destroyed it just as quickly.

"You've got to stay away from Kenneth, Mom. He's bad news, and he will hurt you if given half the chance." She reached out to grasp her hands.

"Oh, honey. Kenneth doesn't want to hurt me. He wants me all to himself. It's you he wants to hurt, and I can't let him do that." Fingers touched her face, pushing some hair out of the way.

"What do you mean?"

"He's making plans, Sasha. Plans that keep you out of the picture and take you away from me and here. I came with him in the hope of seeing you settled and happy, but I know he won't leave you alone completely.

The moment I saw you with, Pussy, I knew you were finally safe, but Kenneth won't stop until you're gone. You're a lot braver than I am." Her mother tightened her grip. "You've got to stay away from Kenneth now. He's dangerous, and he will try to get what he wants."

"Which is why neither of you are leaving this clubhouse," Pussy said.

His voice came somewhere in front of her.

"What did you hear?" she asked.

"All of it. You're going to need to tell me exactly what you told Sasha, and I'm going to need to know it all."

Her mother stood, moving away from her.

"Wait, please don't do this without me."

"The rest of the club, do they need to hear this?" Pussy asked.

"Only if they think they can help. I don't want anything bad happening to my daughter. She's been through enough." Sasha felt her mother's hands shake. They were getting worse with every moment that passed. "I'm going to need to go to rehab. I've got a serious problem, and I'm not strong enough to get through this."

"We'll help you." There was some more movement. "Baby, I'm going to touch you and help you walk downstairs. Are you okay with that?"

"Yes. I'm okay."

"Go on ahead of us," Pussy said.

She heard the door opening, and the footsteps started to fade. "You can't marry me, Pussy."

"Why can't I?"

"Today must have shown you that I'm a bad choice. I couldn't protect anyone. I'm blind, and you need someone strong." She hated saying the words, and the thought of losing Pussy over it was tearing her apart.

He cupped her face, tilting her head back. "Now

you listen to me, Sasha. We're going to get married. You're going to become my wife, and you're going to do that because you love me. I don't give a fuck about you being able to take care of yourself. That's my job. I'll take care of you."

"Pussy?" She went to complain. He silenced her with his lips.

His tongue plundered her mouth.

Moaning, she circled her arms around his neck, loving the feel of his hard body pressed against hers. He slid his fingers into her hair, tightening on the strands. "So fucking beautiful," he said, muttering against her lips. "Now, no more talk of what you can and can't do. I don't need a protector, Sasha."

"I want to be everything you need."

"You are. Believe me, you're more than you think you are." He rubbed his nose against hers. "Stop stressing out. Come on, we need to get out of here and join the others before I fuck you again."

She liked the thought of him fucking her more than going to discuss Kenneth. Her stepfather always ruined the fun. Sasha hated his intrusion in her life. There were times she truly believed she'd never get him out of her life.

Pussy took the lead, holding her hand and moving her downstairs. She held onto the banister and his hand like they were lifelines, which they were. Slowly, she moved downstairs with his aid.

She heard the rumbling of voices as they were all talking. Some were laughing, while others clearly didn't find anything amusing.

Once they were inside the room, silence fell.

"Come on then. I've not got all day to listen to this," Devil said. "My woman is tucked up in bed because of your fucking husband."

119

Sasha winced, wanting to go to her mother.

"Don't. She needs to realize how bad he is." Pussy held her tight to him. His fingers stroked her stomach through her clothing. She loved the way he touched her. He moved his touch to under her shirt. Pussy touched skin, and she felt like electricity had exploded all over her body. Closing her eyes, she tried to focus on what was happening in front of her. She couldn't. His touch took her mind away from the problems they were all facing.

She wished they were alone and she'd get to touch him without fear of anyone watching.

"Tell us what's going on," Devil said. His harsh voice cut through her fantasy bringing her straight back to the reality of her situation.

"I don't know everything."

"Then tell us what you do know," Death said.

Sasha was getting good at recognizing people by their voices alone.

"Kenneth's planning his retirement. He's getting all the funding together so that he doesn't have to worry about money at all." Her mother sighed. "He's planning on having Sasha killed so that he can take me with him. The blindness upped the stakes for him as she can meet an accident without anyone knowing the truth. The last four years have been a façade. He's been showing the town how loving and loyal he is toward Sasha so no one would ever suspect him of killing her or organizing for her to be hit. I heard him talking to Frederick, the guy outside. He's got some paperwork to finish filling out, and then he can leave. Frederick gets the main seat on the Piston County chair, funds the town—"

"And turns it into his own backyard of distribution," Devil said, finishing off her mother's sentence.

"I don't know what's going on. I really wish I did, but I don't. I only know that Kenneth has organized the sale of over ten warehouses in the surrounding area of Piston County," her mother said.

"He's taking over the entire town," Ripper said.

There was silence after that.

"Guys, take your women away. We need to make a call and then deal with the problem at hand," Devil said.

"Come on, baby. Don't fight me on this." Pussy took her hand, leading her back upstairs.

"It's bad, isn't it?" Sasha asked. She didn't need to be able to see to understand bad shit was going to happen.

"Yes, it's bad. I've got to go and deal with this. Your mother will take care of you. Have a bath, relax, soak, and I'll be up when it's all over." Pussy opened his door, leading her inside.

"I didn't want to cause trouble," her mother said.

"You're not. You're helping us. We're going to help you. You're not going to die, and we're not going to let Kenneth take my woman away. I'll kill the bastard myself before I let that happen." He kissed her cheek. "Stay here. Don't leave."

The door closed behind him, leaving her alone.

"He seems like a good man. Everyone believes they're monsters, but they're not. They're all good men, I see it." Her mother kept talking.

"I love him, Mom."

"Good, because I've got a feeling he's in love with you."

"No, he's not. Pussy doesn't do love. I don't mind."

"Honey, you can't see him to know what he's like when he's looking at you. Believe me, he's in love with you, and he's not going to let anything happen to you."

Sasha wanted to argue but decided against it. She liked the thought of him being in love with her.

****

Frederick stared out of his hotel room sipping a glass of expensive brandy. Everything was coming together. Soon he'd own the states from Piston County through to Fort Wills. He already had a stake in Vegas as well. Ned Walker, Eva's father, was going to be next on his list. No one was going to be able to touch him. He'd have the cops, the Feds, and any type of government agency eating out of the palm of his hand because they couldn't do a single thing to stop him.

Tiny, Devil, and Ned were all cogs in this world. They were big in their own little towns and cities, but when it came to the big leagues, they were still little fishes who could be squashed. Frederick had watched them for years, pretending to know the kind of shit they needed to in order to get by. Little drug runs here or there, a few bonus hits on the stock market to keep funds flowing legally.

He knew the real way to make money was through fear. No one knew how to challenge him as there was nothing he held dear. The women he fucked were a convenience that he used to scratch an itch. When he was done with women, he either gave them to business associates as part of a deal or got one of his men to kill them.

For many years he'd wondered about taking over this place. He'd watched many people try and fail to take over Fort Wills and then try to take out Chaos Bleeds and The Skulls. Everyone failed to do anything or even put a dent in their lives.

It was a challenge that he could no longer turn down. Tiny and Devil could be beaten, and he was going to show them all how to do it.

"Boss, what's going on?" Ronald asked.

Frederick smiled. "Nothing is going on. We're going to be setting up business in a matter of time."

"I've got word that Tiny's planning on taking out your guy in the force. The one you're paying to make life difficult," Ronald said.

"That's fine. I've got plans in place for everyone." Frederick sipped at his drink.

"What do you mean?"

"For every person Tiny or Devil kill, one of their own will die. Tiny lays a hand on my men, he loses one of his men, his wife, or his kid. Murphy and Tate seem like a good target." He smiled thinking about the brass bitch that was Tiny's spawn. "Let him attack. The moment he does, I click a button, and he loses one. I don't know when or how, but it will be soon."

He'd put everything in place. His men were all around Piston County and Fort Wills. No one knew when he'd strike. Chaos Bleeds and The Skulls were ending with him. Frederick was going to show all the people who had failed that it was in fact possible to own the two towns. It just took careful planning to get the job done.

Chapter Nine

"What are you trying to say?" Tiny asked. They had The Skulls on speaker phone, and all the crew was present to hear it.

"Frederick is screwing with us. This is not about taking over as a partner or even as a business. He's going to get rid of us, Tiny." Devil ran a hand over his face. Pussy's president looked tired and worn out with this latest revelation.

"How do you know this woman heard the truth? For all you know her hearing is as bad as her choices."

Letting out a sigh, Pussy saw all of his brothers agreed with Tiny. "She's drugged and addicted to alcohol, but she loves her daughter, Tiny. I'll vouch for her. She's telling the truth about Kenneth." He looked at all of the men. "Didn't you guys see it in Kenneth's eyes? He threw a brick through a window. If he's not got something planned then I'm a fucking idiot. There is more to this than meets the eye."

"I fucked up, and we're all dealing with Frederick," Curse said. "I don't think this is anything other than a business relationship. We can't control what a stepfather wants to do. This is being blown out of proportion."

"He killed Ashley. She was a business partner to us," Pussy said.

"She was also gathering information for us," Devil said, speaking up. "Tiny, I'm telling you, man, trust me on this. We're going to regret letting this lie if you don't believe me."

"You've not actually said anything," Tiny said.

"He's going to kill us all." Devil's words rang throughout the whole room.

"What?" Pussy asked, frowning. When did that

conclusion get jumped to? Pussy liked living. He'd only just found Sasha, and he wasn't going to die trying.

"Think about it. He starts here with Curse taking out that fucker Dale. We're doing the transport shit of his business, moving whatever he wants. Then, he just happens to come to Fort Wills. Butch's past with him. This has got to have been planned, Tiny. Frederick Gonzalez is not looking to do business with two small MCs. We don't have the manpower that he needs." Devil was pacing the office. "Where he comes from we're two little fish in a whole fucking ocean. He doesn't want us. He wants the towns that link us all up in between."

"Where are you going with this, boss?" Death asked.

"Frederick has a plan. He's too intelligent not to have a plan. Think about it. What do you do when you can own part of a state?"

"You take out the competition and set up shop." Tiny spoke up over the line.

"This has nothing to do with us. Frederick is gaining ground on our soil. He's setting up shops, warehouses, distribution, girls, guns. You name it, he's running it. All of us will be in his pocket. We're expendable, and no one can do anything about it."

"For all of those who feel a little slow, raise your hand and ask how he can do this?" Snake asked.

"He's not running it. Frederick has a lot of little people, like us, to get caught. We're expendable, and when he no longer needs us, he pops us off," Pussy said. "He's playing cat and mouse, only we're the mouse and he's the cat that's hiding in the long grass out by the field waiting to catch us one by one."

Devil nodded. "He's got the means of putting us away for a long time. Our families are in danger, Tiny. We've got to come up with a plan to take this fucker out.

I'm sick and tired of waiting."

"Alex has gone to Vegas. Ned's fighters are being attacked, Devil. Whatever is happening, he's going after Ned now as well." Tiny sounded awful. "Fuck, this is getting complicated."

"We'll meet up, and we'll talk it out," Devil said.

"Yeah, I think we should come to you this time. Something is going on in Fort Wills. I don't trust a meeting here. We'll come to you, and we'll talk then." Tiny hung up the phone.

Frowning, Pussy saw Devil wasn't expecting that.

"What's that all about?" Pussy asked.

"I don't know. Until further notice I want you all to stick to the clubhouse. All of us are staying around. I don't want to risk one of us dying because I wasn't cautious enough with you all," Devil said, looking at each of them in turn.

They all nodded. As they made their way out of the office, Pussy stayed behind to speak to Devil.

"What's the matter?" Devil asked, when they were both alone.

"I'm going to kill Homer when I next see him."

Devil looked up at him. "Good."

"You're not going to argue with me. Tell me that I need to keep my shit together because of Gonzalez?" Pussy folded his arms. He knew Devil, had served with the Chaos Bleeds crew for a long time.

"No, I'm not."

"Why?"

"Because Gonzalez never had any intention of keeping Ashley alive. I should have seen it. However, I was trying to make sure our club stayed alive long enough to deal with him. He's upped the ante on our lives. I'm not going to allow him to take over our town, ruin my club, and hurt my woman. We're going to fight back, if it's the last thing I do for this club."

Devil stared back at him.

"Are you going to take out Kenneth?"

"The fucker threw a brick at my clubhouse, and it hit my woman. Kenneth's on borrowed time. For the past few months we've been acting like a bunch of pussies facing off the school bully." Devil took a deep breath and smiled. "I hate bullies. I've never liked them. It's time for us to be grown ass men. We're not sitting down and taking shit anymore. Frederick can go and fuck himself if he thinks I'm some kind of lapdog. I suggest you do the same."

Devil walked past him, leaving him stood alone in the office. Glancing around the office, Pussy finally felt free. For the past few months they'd been trying to deal with Gonzalez's demands whereas now, they were going to take the fight to him.

He breathed easier. Closing the office door, he headed up to his room. Opening the door he found Sasha's mother tapping her leg. She needed to go somewhere as otherwise it was going to get a whole lot messier.

"Death." His friend was the one who organized the rehabilitation centers.

"This better be fucking good," Death said, pulling up his jeans as he exited the room three doors down.

"Pussy, what's going on?" Sasha asked.

Ignoring his woman, he motioned for her mother to come to him. She got off the floor and walked toward him. She was pale, sweating, and looked ready to throw up.

"You're the only who handles admissions. She needs rehab, and you need to get her there tonight," Pussy said.

"Shit, this fucking sucks. I'll get Curse to come

with me as backup."

Pussy didn't give Sasha time to say goodbye to her mother. It wouldn't be long before she was back home with them. Pussy watched as Death led her mother away with Curse in tow. The two men were going to be pissed at him, but he didn't care. He wasn't leaving his woman alone tonight.

"Pussy, what's going on?" she asked.

"We've sent your mother to rehab. The pills and alcohol have taken their toll, and in order for us to keep her around, she needs to be clean. We're all clean, baby. Devil made sure the whole club got clean with this shit with Gonzalez." Pussy removed his jacket and kicked off his shoes.

She wore one of his shirts with a skull-and-crossbones on the front. With her hair wild around her face, she looked so fucking sexy.

"Baby, I need to take a shower." He stepped closer to her, taking hold of her hand. "Come with me."

He liked the way she held him a little tighter as she walked. Pussy knew she needed to hold him because of her inability to see. Her eyes were focused in front of her as she stood up. Over time, he hoped these little actions would help her build up her confidence. He'd already decided he was going to get her a dog to help her.

There was no way he'd let her go without while she could have the independence she clearly craved.

"I've already taken a shower."

"Now, you're going to take another shower as I want to see your body naked. It has been too long since I saw your tits."

She gasped. "I'm never going to get used to this."

"Baby, you're not going to have a choice. This is who I am. I like to curse and to say shit the way I see it. Your tits are mine, and so is this beautiful pussy." He didn't release her hand as he reached behind him and flicked on the shower. Cold water cascaded in the tub. Moving away, he drew the shirt she wore up over her head.

Sasha wasn't wearing any panties. He had a clear view of her perfect pussy that he'd trimmed and shaved to perfection.

Placing both of her hands on his stomach, he removed his jeans and told her what he was doing at the same time.

Her fingers danced across his skin. When they were both naked, he tugged her into the shower, helping her inside.

She giggled, wrapping her arms around his neck. The water fell over each of them, slicking their bodies.

"I can't wait anymore to kiss you." He dropped his head down, licking the path along her lips. She didn't leave him waiting long as she moaned, opening her lips.

Plundering her mouth, he tasted her.

She was everything he hoped she'd be, and he didn't want to let her go.

****

Pussy's hands stayed on Sasha's hips as his tongue played inside her mouth. Heat spilled between her legs. Wrapping her arms around his neck she tried to pull him closer to feel him pressed to her body. There was nothing stopping him from taking her.

She wanted his rock hard cock thrusting inside her.

He was turning her into a sex maniac. All her thoughts zeroed in on the pleasure he could give her with his hands and mouth.

"Please," she said.

"Touch me, Sasha. I don't want you to move your hands away from me." He spoke the words against her lips. Running her hands up and down his body, she tried to memorize the feel of him by touch. "Here." He took her palm, placing it on his cheek.

Taking her time, she touched his face, learning the contours and beauty of him. Caressing his lips, she smiled. "I love these."

He didn't say anything. She winced at the word she'd used.

Get used to not saying it.

No, she wouldn't. She loved Pussy, and there was no way she'd hide it from him. Sliding a thumb into his mouth she giggled. "I love the way you lick my pussy, Shane."

She used his name just like he asked her to.

"Woman, you're going to drive me crazy. Where have you come from?"

"I'm away from danger. You make me feel safe, and I can tell you the truth about what I wa—" Sasha was cut off by his lips. His tongue slid inside her mouth, and she caressed his with her own.

He tasted amazing, and she didn't want it to end.

"You've no idea what you do to me," he said.

She was starting to get an idea. He was driving her crazy as well.

Licking her lips, she moved her hands down to his chest. Spreading her palms out, she fingered his nipples. They budded against her fingers, and she released a moan.

"That's it, baby. Touch me."

Leaning forward, she flicked one bud with her tongue. His hands sank into her hair, but he didn't pull her away.

Sucking his nipple into her mouth, she kissed along his chest until she gave his other nipple the same attention.

Pussy moaned, the sounds vibrating through his body letting her know she was doing everything right for him. With her mouth busy, she glided her hands down learning each ripple and ridge. He was a strong man. His body showed how much he worked out.

"That's right, baby. Touch me."

Down she went until she encountered the thick length of his cock. Pausing at his stomach, she circled the base of his cock, working her fingers up to the tip. He was long, hard, and thick. She didn't need to see to know this.

"Fuck." The hand in her hair tightened. She loved the slight pain he caused as she was giving him pleasure. Smiling, she lowered herself to her knees.

"What the fuck are you doing?"

"I want to do with you what you did to me. I'm going to suck your cock and give you just as much pleasure as you did me." She worked from base to the tip, sliding her hand up and down the shaft.

He released his hold on her hair. Pressing her mouth to her hand, she worked out where the tip of his cock was. Flicking her tongue over the head, she tasted something musky and salty.

"What's that?" she asked.

"It's my cum. I'm turned on, and it leaks out of the tip." He cursed again as she sucked the very tip of his cock into her mouth. She loved the taste of him instantly.

Moaning, she took more of him until he hit the back of her throat. With her free hand, she reached down to touch herself.

"Are you fingering your clit?" he asked.

She murmured her answer.

"Fuck, you're so fucking perfect."

The water washed down around them. Using one hand at the base of his shaft, she worked up a pace that meant she didn't gag on his length. With her other hand, she touched her clit, sliding a finger over the bud then down to her cunt to press inside her.

She'd never touched herself. Sucking Pussy's cock, she took her time to get to know her own body. Sasha learned what she liked, using two fingers to rub her clit.

"You're so fucking sexy. When I get you in my bed I'm going to taste your pussy. I'm going to fill you up with my cum."

All of his dirty words drove her closer to orgasm. She didn't want to come before him.

"Give me those fucking fingers," he said.

Holding her hand up, she felt his large hand circle her wrist. The heat of his mouth swamped her fingers, sucking them into his mouth. She moaned at the small contact. His mouth would be so warm sucking on her clit.

Bobbing on his shaft, she took more of him to the back of her throat. When she couldn't handle anymore, she pulled away to circle the tip. She loved his pre-cum and wanted more. Licking the tip, she moaned as each new taste exploded on her tongue.

"Fuck, baby, keep playing with your cunt. I want more."

She slid her fingers inside her pussy then brought them up to tease her clit. Each glide over her nub had her almost coming. There was no way she was going to be able to hold off her orgasm.

"That's it, baby, come over your fingers."

With no other choice, she released his cock and gasped out as her orgasm crashed through her. Crying out, she continued to finger her clit.

Pussy took her, sliding his fingers through her slit. "So fucking beautiful." Kneeling in the tub, she fucked herself onto his hand, never wanting it to end.

When she couldn't handle anymore, she gripped his wrist and begged him to stop.

"Enough, please. I can't handle anymore."

He paused, moving his hand out of her hold. She heard him sucking on his fingers.

He helped her to her feet. Her legs were like jelly as he moved her.

"No, please, I want to give you an orgasm."

"Baby, you can give me an orgasm soon."

Shaking her head, she tried to go back to her knees.

"Sasha, no. I need to be inside you before the end of the night." He lifted her up in his arms and turned the shower off.

His strength surprised her. Holding onto him, she tried to think of where he was moving her.

Pussy eased her on the bed. He kissed her mouth, and he was moving down her body, sucking on her nipples in turn. There was no stopping him as he went down, pressing kisses to every inch of her body.

He opened her thighs, and then she screamed as he attacked her clit, sucking the bud into his mouth.

"Pussy, stop."

"Why?"

"I've come."

"So? I want you to come again and not to stop." He flicked his tongue repeatedly over her clit. She fisted her hands in the sheets as the pleasure took on a whole new feeling. Every part of her body was alive, sensitive to the smallest touch. She didn't know if she'd survive through another orgasm.

His fingers held onto her hips as he thrust his tongue into her core. The pleasure built within her, drawing her closer and closer.

"I can feel you, baby. You're so close to letting go. Give me your orgasm."

She didn't know how it was possible, but only a few flicks of his tongue and she hurtled into another orgasm that was much better than the last one. Her fingers were nothing compared to his talented tongue.

He gripped her hand, and she sank her nails into the flesh.

Pussy moved up the bed.

"How was that, baby?" he asked.

"I can't feel my body." She felt like she was floating. Her head was pounding, and she breathed out a sigh. "That was amazing."

"You better get used to amazing," he said.

His arms ran across her body. She stroked his arm, loving how safe he made her feel.

"I love you." She snuggled in against him, knowing she wanted more.

"I love you, too," he said, taking her by surprise.

"What?" She tensed up in shock.

"Tell me about it, baby. It took me completely by surprise."

She shook her head. "You told me you didn't do love."

"I didn't until I met you. I guess you made me change my mind." His fingers teased down to graze the skin at the top of her pussy.

"You're in love with me? You're being serious."

"I don't joke about shit like this, Sasha. I love you. I want to marry you."

She stayed silent, unsure what to actually say to him.

"You don't believe me?"

"Erm, no, I don't. I'm sorry. It just seems a little hard to believe that you'd change your mind within a matter of hours."

He'd never given her a reason to doubt him, yet she didn't trust his sudden change. Why would he change his mind so quickly?

"I lost one of my best friends because I didn't protect her. She paid the price for the club's mistake. I hate being vulnerable, and with you, I am. It's not because of you. Ever since I first met you there's been something different about you. I can't focus when I'm around you. All I want to do is sit and watch you."

His words were so touching. She wanted him to stop and yet continue on talking.

"Seeing Kenneth with you angered me. I knew that fucker was an evil bastard, but I just didn't know how much." He tensed beside her, dropping a kiss to her shoulder. "I'll never let anything happen to you again. You're mine to love and to protect. I'm not going to hide my feelings from you anymore, Sasha. I own you now."

"I'm not something to be owned."

"You're mine, and I promise you, I'll protect you until the day I die."

He didn't say anything else. She smiled. At last, she knew what it was like to finally be wanted by a man. Nothing else could harm or hurt her with Pussy in her life.

Chapter Ten

Pussy gave Sasha time to allow his words to sink in. He wasn't letting her go, and it wasn't just because of Kenneth. From the first moment he saw her, he'd been struck by her beauty. Kenneth had been hurting her then as well, showing his power over her with everyone watching. Every chance the bastard got, he'd made her more and more dependent on him. Pussy wasn't going to let her feel vulnerable. He had every intention of showing her how powerful she was in life without depending on everyone.

In the weeks to come he intended to find them a house, a nice one without any stairs for her to master. There would be no fear for her to encounter anymore.

Devil would kill Kenneth, Pussy was sure of it. His boss wouldn't allow the pain caused to Lexie to slide.

There were going to be repercussions for their actions. The Chaos Bleeds crew was back, and he felt stronger, knowing they weren't going to get butt fucked by this man.

"I'm going to fuck you now," he said.

He'd mentioned filling her up with his cum. Pussy knew he couldn't do that at the moment. He wasn't ready to father any child. With Kenneth's control, there was no way she'd be on any birth control.

"Yes, please," she said.

"I'm just getting a condom." He left the bed, opening up his drawer. Retrieving the condom, he saw a picture of Ashley staring up at him. It was one of him with Ashley and Mia. The picture was taken at the diner. He remembered Ashley pulling Mia down into her lap. Curse took the shot before the shit hit the fan. They'd all been happy for a short time. *I'm sorry, Ash. I hope you can forgive me.*

He'd loved her like a friend. Grabbing the condom, he closed the drawer and turned back to his woman. There would be time for revenge soon enough. Until then, he was going to enjoy the feel of his woman coming on his shaft.

Tearing into the latex, he slid the condom over his rock hard shaft. The memory of her sweet lips wrapped around his dick made him harder than a rock.

With time he'd teach her exactly how he liked to have his cock sucked. She was already doing a brilliant job without his interference.

Stepping to the bottom of the bed, he stared up the length of her body. She had curves in all the right places. From the first view of her, he'd fallen for her. No other woman could ever have this kind of effect over him.

"Open your legs," he said. "I want to see that pretty pussy of mine."

She moaned but opened her thighs showing him her cunt. The lips of her pussy were open, and her cum glistened on the lips of her sex. Climbing onto the bed, he kept his gaze on her pussy. Moving up her body, he gripped his cock, positioned himself at her entrance, and slid deeply inside her. Her cunt clenched around his shaft each inch that he went inside her.

Her hands gripped his arms. Staring into her brown eyes, he saw they were wide with wonder. Her blindness didn't bother him; it never had. Learning of her impairment and the cause, he'd been driven insane with worry over her safety.

No more worrying as she was going to be his wife and his reason for breathing.

Seating to the hilt within her warmth, he wrapped his arms around her body, pulling out then slamming back inside. He took possession of her mouth as he slowly fucked her body, taking them both into pleasure.

Gripping her hands, he ordered her to fuck him back. She arched up against him, meeting him thrust for thrust. Keeping her hands locked beside her head, he slammed deep, speeding up his thrusts.

She cried out, gasping. Her tight pussy clenched around every inch inside her. Staring down at his latex covered cock, he watched himself going in and out of her hole. It was so fucking pretty he almost came at the sight alone.

Pulling out of her body, he turned her onto her knees.

"What are you doing?"

"I'm going to take you in my favorite position. I get to fuck you from behind and play with your ass." He found her core and pressed inside once again. The different angle meant he went deeper.

He watched her hands tighten on the pillow she was holding. Pussy wasn't going to stop. He wanted to hear her screaming out in pleasure from his cock alone.

Running his fingers down her back, he felt her shake beneath him.

"Do you like what I'm doing to you?" he asked.

"I feel full. You're, erm, bigger."

Pussy chuckled. "Get used to it, baby."

Following down to the curves of her ass, he spread the cheeks wide. The puckered hole glinted up at him. Staring down, he saw her pussy gripping his cock as well as felt her clench around him. It was all a heady experience.

Pulling out of her warmth, he watched the slick condom reappear. He couldn't wait to see his dick without a condom inside her.

He stroked her clit, coating his fingers in her cum.

She moaned, jerking against him, and her pussy got tighter around his cock.

Once his fingers were slick with cum, he pressed them to her asshole. She tensed beneath him.

"It's okay, baby. Everything I do to you, you'll love. Trust me."

Slowly, she started to relax as he teased her anus. He pressed the tip of one finger against her entrance, waiting for her to open up.

Pumping in and out of her cunt, he kept applying pressure until her tight ring of muscles let him inside. Pushing his finger inside her, he took his time, letting her get accustomed to the feel of him.

She began to push back against him, taking more and more of his cock within her pussy.

Soon, he was adding a second finger to her ass, opening her up and spreading her wide.

Over and over, he worked her cunt and ass, feeling her ripple around him. With his other hand, he teased her clit. She shattered around his cock with a few strokes of his fingers.

Her sweet cries were amazing to hear. All he wanted to do was have her climaxing over him.

"You're so perfect," he said, driving in deep to find his own climax. Within three strokes, he spilled his cum into the condom. Groaning, he gripped her hip, knowing he was in heaven with her. Nothing else mattered in his life so long as Sasha was with him.

Turning her to her side, he collapsed on the bed, banding a hand around her waist.

"I'll clean us up in a moment. I want to hold you."

His cock was still buried inside her cunt. The pleasure was intense, and there was no stopping the love he felt for her. The love he felt for her was as natural as breathing. She took over all of his senses, making it hard to deal with anything else.

"I love you, baby."

"I'm never going to get tired of hearing you say that to me," she said, chuckling.

"Good. We're going to need to get washed up in a moment."

"I can't believe you played with my ass."

She was too innocent.

"Wait until I fuck it."

Sasha tensed, causing him to chuckle.

"Don't worry. I'll have you all prepared before I sink my cock into your hot little ass." He kissed her neck, breathing in her scent. "How did I get so fucking lucky having you?"

"I'm the lucky one," she said. He opened his eyes as she turned her head toward him. "I never thought it could be this amazing."

"It can get better. You won't have to worry about your stepfather and mother. He'll be out of the picture, and your mother will be taken care of." He kissed her cheek.

"Thank you."

"You're an old lady now, Sasha. Your needs will all come first." He nuzzled her neck.

The door slammed open, and Pussy jerked out of her, putting his fists up ready to fight whoever charged into the room.

It was Ripper.

"You're needed downstairs. A hit went out on Tate and Murphy an hour ago. She's in the hospital and may not wake up. Curse and Death are still not back, and no one can get them on their cells. Devil wants us all for a meeting."

Pussy nodded, lowering his hands. "Get the fuck

out of my room. I'll be down in a moment."

Once the door was closed, he walked into the bathroom, washing his hands and getting rid of the condom. He went back into the room. Sasha was sat up on the bed, staring at the floor.

"Is it bad? I've never heard of a Tate and Murphy."

"They're part of The Skulls. Tate is Tiny's oldest daughter. If this hit went out then everyone is fucked." He cleaned between her thighs. "I'm going to ask you to stay in bed. I don't need to be worrying about you when club business is about to go down."

"What about my mom? Death and Curse took her, didn't they? How come no one has heard anything?" she asked, panicking.

"I'll get Lexie to stop by. You've got to stop worrying, as otherwise you're going to start losing your mind." He leaned down, kissing her temple. "Please, stop worrying. I'll find your mother. You wouldn't want any of them answering the phone while they're on their bikes, would you?" he asked.

She shook her head.

He wasn't about to tell her that they'd gone in a car. Kissing her head a final time, he eased out of the room. Walking up the flight of stairs, he knocked on Devil's door. Lexie answered, looking tired. She held Elizabeth in her arms. "Could you go and sit with Sasha? She's panicking."

"Is it true? They can't reach Curse and Death?"

"I don't know for sure. It's what Ripper told me. Her mother was traveling with them. I'd appreciate it if you didn't mention anything to her."

"I won't. You can't keep something like this from her, Pussy," Lexie said, gripping Simon's hand as she made the way out of the room.

"I know. I don't want to worry her until I have to."

He charged downstairs to find the rest of his brothers stood in the main room. Devil was on the phone, pacing the room. "We're taking them down whether you like it or not. I'm not going to be afraid of shit." Devil hung up, looking at each of them.

"What's going on?" Ripper asked.

"Tiny decided to pay a little visit to the fucker who hurt his woman. The cop who raided the clubhouse a couple of months ago. Within ten minutes a hit was ordered on Tate. They were traveling back from the shopping center with groceries. The car was rained with bullets. Their son came out of it unscathed. Murphy was shot in the shoulder. He lost control of the car, and Tate in her panic released the seatbelt to protect their son. She's in a coma, and it's not looking good." Devil threw his cell phone. The device landed on the floor, shattering at their feet. "This is it. I mean it, boys. I'm done playing this game."

Folding his arms, Pussy stared at his boss, waiting to see what was going to happen.

"We're the Chaos Bleeds crew, and it's time to end this peace-keeping shit we've been doing."

"What about Curse and Death? Where are they?"

"They're at the rehab center. Someone tried to whack them. They killed the guy and called me the moment it was done," Devil said.

Pussy breathed out a sigh of relief.

"Gonzalez has taken one of our own from us. He killed Ashley, and he killed Jerry in front of us. He thinks he's better than us. It's time to show him how fucking little he actually is."

Nodding, Pussy was ready. He was more than ready.

"Tomorrow, we're riding out, and we're going to start a fucking war with this asshole." Devil looked at all of them. "Tonight, you go to your woman. You make love to her, you fuck her, because tomorrow, we may not be coming home."

The war had just begun, and Pussy couldn't wait to take his vengeance on the bastard who'd put them in this position.

****

"How can you stand these private meetings?" Sasha asked.

Lexie sat on the bed with her two children sleeping beside her. When she entered, Lexie helped her to dress, making little Simon stare at the wall.

"You learn not to care about what they're doing."

Sasha heard the fear in Lexie's voice.

"What's going on?"

"If you can't stand them having meetings like this, then you're not going to like what I've got to say."

"Please, tell me. I don't like being kept in the dark. I've got enough darkness already."

Lexie sighed. "Devil is a strong man. He's a force to be reckoned with." She stopped for a moment. "He'll kill whoever poses a threat. This guy, this Gonzalez guy, came in, and it broke the club a little. My man's been fighting to get himself back."

"Has he?"

"The brick that was thrown at me, it has woken him up. Devil's going to pick a fight, and I don't know if he intends to come home alive," Lexie said.

The door opened. "Devil's waiting for you, Lex," Pussy said.

"Can you help me with the kids, Pussy? I've not got the energy to move them."

"Sure."

Sasha listened to them moving around, wishing she could help. She stayed on the bed until Pussy returned.

"What's going on?" she asked.

"Devil's taking the fight to Gonzalez. We're heading out tomorrow. You're going to stay here until I get back." He joined her on the bed.

She felt his body was naked beside her.

"What about my mom?"

"Everything is fine. She checked into the clinic. Death and Curse are going to stay there to make sure everything is safe before they return home."

"They're in danger?"

"Some people want us dead, and we don't want to end up dead. We're going to try to make sure that doesn't happen."

She lay down on his arm, curling against him. "I don't want anything bad to happen to you."

"I won't let it."

"How do you know that?" she asked.

He ran a hand down her back, cupping her ass. "I know that I'll fight to get back to you."

She stroked across his stomach thinking about what he was saying. "Do you have to go?"

"Babe, I've got a score to settle. This Gonzalez bastard needs to learn not to fuck with us or the club. Otherwise bad shit's going to happen."

Sasha moved down to cup his cock. "Is there anything I could do to stop you from going?"

He covered her hand with his. "No, there's not a damn thing you can do. I love you, Sasha, and I'm going to do everything in my power to get back to you. I need to do this, and you're going to have to support me."

"Is this about Ashley?" she asked, working from the base up to the root.

"Yes. I need some closure on her. I need to do this."

She understood his need more than he realized. "Okay, you'll come back to me?"

His fingers touched her cheek. "Baby, I'll come back to you, and you'll be fighting to get rid of me. I'm never going to let anything happen to any of us. We're going to start a fight and do what we do best."

"And what's that?" she asked.

"Cause a little chaos. It's how we got our name, and it's time for others to remember that shit." He dropped a kiss to her lips. "Now, are we going to talk some more, or can I fuck you?"

She gasped.

"That's right, Sasha. You're my woman, and I need to fuck you and memorize every inch of your body before I leave."

How could she deny such a request?

"Please, Pussy."

"What did I tell you to call me?" he asked.

"Shane, please, Shane, fuck me."

"That's better." He pushed her to the bed and slid between her thighs. She reached up, and he placed her palms against his chest. "I want you to touch me."

She caressed his body as he sucked on her nipples. The smallest touch had her heart racing. The pleasure crashed through her whole body, and she thrust up to meet him.

"Not yet, baby. I'm not even inside you." His palm landed on her stomach, keeping her still.

Dropping her hands away from him, she cried out as he bit down onto her nipple.

"Please!"

"When I'm ready." He growled the words against her skin.

The sounds he made turned her on more. She found his head and sank her fingers into the strands, loving the feel of him against her.

He moved from one nipple to the other, lavishing attention.

There was no way she'd be able to survive the onslaught of her pleasure his mouth was creating.

"Fuck, I've got to take you now. I can't wait for a fucking condom."

Pussy reached down to grasp his cock. She felt the tip of his shaft bump her clit before sliding down to her entrance. "You're so fucking wet already."

He made her this way. His body, the words he spoke, all turned her on.

"Please, I need you," she said.

In one smooth thrust, he slammed deep within her body. She cried out arching up to get closer, deeper.

"Shh, I've got you, Sasha. I'm never going to let go." He took hold of her hands, pressing them to the bed. "I'm going to fuck you, and I'm not going to stop until we're both screaming in pleasure. Do you have a problem with that?"

"No, no problem." With the thick length of his cock inside her she couldn't think about anything else. He filled her completely leaving no room to think of anything other than him. She felt the way he pulsed inside her. The heat of him was different. There was no rubber holding him away from her or between them.

He pulled all the way out of her until only the tip was inside, and then with one long jerk, he shoved every inch inside her. The pain combined with the pleasure was a heady experience. She locked her fingers with his and enjoyed the ride he was taking her on.

Over and over, he pulled out only to slam inside. Each stroke was precise, prolonging their pleasure.

"I can feel your pussy clenching around me, baby. It knows who its master is. Do you know who your master is?" he asked.

"Yes."

"Say my name."

"Shane."

"And who am I?" he asked.

Every time he spoke, he thrust inside her.

"You're my master."

"Good girl."

He didn't stop and pounded inside her. She gripped his hands tightly as he rode her body harder than ever before. The depth shocked her, yet she wanted more. Pussy took possession of her lips, sliding his tongue in and out of her mouth.

"You feel so fucking good. Your naked pussy is tightening around me as if it's got a life of its own." He groaned, kissing down to her neck. She tilted her head to the side, and he sucked on the flesh.

She whimpered at the pleasure.

"That's it, baby. Give me everything. Let me hear you come."

He pulled out of her pussy and bumped her clit with his rock hard shaft. She cried out at the jolt of ecstasy.

"Come for me." He released one of her hands, and his fingers replaced his cock. Sasha didn't stand a chance against his latest onslaught.

Her orgasm crashed through her as he pounded away, refusing to release her.

"Fuck, baby, I'm going to come." Within seconds Pussy followed her into bliss.

She felt the jerk of his cock along with the pulse of his cum. Afterward he collapsed against her.

"I love you."

"I love you, too. Please, don't go."

"I've got to go, and you're going to have to trust me with this." He kissed her lips. "I've not broken a single promise I've made to you, have I?"

She shook her head.

"I'm not going to start now."

Sasha hoped everything was going to be okay. In all of her life she'd never known any man about to go and start a fight. Especially a fight he didn't know he could win.

****

"You shouldn't go," Lexie said. "It's dangerous."

"I've taken this guy's shit, Lex. For the past few months I've been living with his fucking demands. I'm a bastard postal service, and if we get caught, that's it." Devil sat naked on the bed. Their children were asleep in the room next to theirs. He stared at his woman, seeing her in tight night shorts and a thin strap shirt. She looked so fucking sexy, and seeing her like this made his dick ache to be inside her. "Come here."

She stepped closer to him. Pushing her shorts out of the way, he eased his cock inside her pussy. Lexie wrapped her legs around his waist, as he slid in deep. He wasn't wearing a condom, and they'd been trying for another baby.

"I'm scared."

"Don't be." He pushed the straps of her shirt underneath her breasts. Watching those lush mounds bounce as he fucked her always drove him insane.

Whatever she was about to say was cut off by a moan.

"You and the kids mean the world to me, Lex. I'm not going to let this fucker take shit away from us anymore. He can take me away, the kids, you. I can't let that happen. This is going to stop him from doing that."

He cupped her cheek, feeling her pussy clench around him. "When it comes to you I'll never take any risks."

"I love you, Devil. You've got to promise me you'll come back to me. I didn't agree to doing this on my own."

"I'm not asking you to. We're going to be a team all the way." He sank his fingers into her hair, tugging on the full strands. Her tits arched up toward him. "Now shut the fuck up so I can fuck you."

"Is my man back?"

"I've never been gone." He plundered her mouth as he ravished her pussy.

He was back, and no one was going to be telling him what to do. This was his club, his town, and everyone could go and fuck themselves.

If Frederick thought he could fuck with Devil then it was time for him to show Frederick what fucking with the Devil of Chaos Bleeds really meant.

Chapter Eleven

Pussy stared at his woman as she stood in the main hall. She was holding onto Judi's arm as she stared at the floor. Wrapping his arms around her, he tilted her head back and claimed her lips. "I'll be back before you know it."

"What should I do?" she asked.

"Call your mother and see how she's settled into the clinic. It won't be long before you don't even recognize her. She's in good hands." He turned to look at Lexie. She was wrapped around Devil wearing his leather cut. Every inch of her displayed her role within the club. She was Devil's old lady and the leader of the women. No one fucked with her unless they wanted shit to come down on their heads. "Lex will take care of you."

"I love you."

"I love you, too, baby." He kissed the top of her head and turned away.

Following his brothers out of the main hall he ignored the sweet-butts as he passed. Ripper stood beside his bike, looking at the clubhouse.

"Are you okay, man?"

"No, I'm not okay. Leaving Judi behind is like wrenching my fucking heart out." Ripper took out a cigarette and lit up. "But I so want a chance to kick this fucker's ass in. We've been pussies for too fucking long. It's time for a little payback, I think."

Pussy couldn't agree more.

"What's happening with Curse and Death?" Pussy asked.

"They're meeting us on the road. Devil's arranged for a meeting near one of Frederick's known warehouses. Our boss is about to start a full out war. I can't wait." Ripper chuckled, throwing his cigarette to the ground. "It's show time."

Devil walked out of the clubhouse going straight for his bike. Some of the club members were staying behind to keep an eye on the clubhouse and the women.

Climbing onto his bike, Pussy stared at his woman as Judi led her out. She looked so beautiful even though she was out of place.

With her face being the last thing he saw Pussy pulled out of the parking lot and followed the rest of his club. Today he'd get his vengeance and the club would be back to being who they were supposed to be.

The drive went by slowly. The sun rose in the sky, and his mind was on the job at hand. The Skulls could sit around waiting for shit to happen. Chaos Bleeds were done waiting. They were taking the fight to the problem.

Time passed, and the ride on his bike relaxed him. He loved being on the open road.

I love Sasha a hell of a lot more.

He smiled thinking about her. She meant so much to him, and yet they'd barely known each other.

Looking ahead of him, Pussy saw the warehouse come into view. Devil pulled into the available parking space set off from the old warehouse that had been used for employees when the warehouse was in use.

Turning his engine off, he saw the cars surrounding Frederick Gonzalez. Kenneth, Homer, and Ronald were clear to see.

Feeling happier, Pussy climbed off his bike going to stand with his president. Death and Curse arrived within minutes. Pussy kept his gaze on Homer and Ronald. Both men looked startled to see the other two alive. Frederick gave no sign of any emotion.

"So what's the meaning of this, Devil?" Frederick

asked.

"I thought it was time for us to have a chat."

"If I wanted a chat I'd have called you."

Devil chuckled. "Yeah, we heard about the hit on Murphy and Tate. You like playing games, don't you?"

"There are no games going on here, Devil. You're a means to an end. I need you for one thing, transportation. When you fail to be of use, I get rid of you."

Kenneth smirked from his place beside Frederick. "I'm going to be wanting my wife and daughter."

"I've got a problem with you, fuck-face," Devil said, glaring at Kenneth.

"Who the fuck are you talking to?" Kenneth asked, going red in the face.

"Come here and talk to me like that."

Frederick smirked. "Go on, Kenneth. He won't do anything. I need you all alive."

Pussy stared at Homer. In his mind he saw Ashley's laughing face despite her troubled past. She didn't deserve to die. Whatever Devil had planned Pussy wasn't leaving until this fucker was in the ground. Kenneth took the cocky steps toward Devil. The bastard was so sure of his position in Frederick's life.

Smirking, Pussy watched as Devil looked relaxed. His boss always looked most relaxed when he was about to strike and kill.

"What do you want?" Kenneth asked.

"Play nice, Devil. He's a cunt, but I need him for work," Frederick said, glancing down at his cell phone.

For several seconds Devil didn't do anything. He stared at Kenneth, and then in one motion, the blade Devil had been hiding struck in Kenneth's neck. "You hurt my fucking wife, you sick little fuck. You blinded a woman and were going to kill her to get her out of the way. You're fucking dead."

Ronald and Homer tensed up. Drawing his gun, Pussy aimed it at Homer while the rest of his brothers aimed guns at Frederick and Ronald.

"I wouldn't fucking think about it."

"This about the black haired bitch, Ashley?" Homer asked.

Pussy didn't respond. He was waiting for his boss to give the go ahead to end this fucker. All he needed was for Devil to say the words and this man was gone.

"I didn't give you permission," Frederick said, getting to his feet.

"I'd sit down if I was you," Curse said. "Nothing would give me more pleasure than seeing you piss and shit yourself before I blow your fucking brains out."

Kenneth gargled, and blood dripped out of his mouth.

"What? You got nothing to say to me?"

Devil chuckled. "Think you can mess with me, think the fuck again." He withdrew the knife then slammed it back inside the side of Kenneth's neck. Over and over Devil struck out at Kenneth leaving a puddle of blood.

"Pussy, now," Devil shouted.

Dropping his gun to the man's cock, Pussy shot Homer's dick off. He fired two more bullets, one in each knee cap, until the man was on the floor, screaming. Gripping him by his head, Pussy tugged his head back and stared into his eyes. These would be the eyes Ashley looked into before she died. This man wouldn't have made it easy for her.

"She ... worth ... it?" Homer asked.

"She was my friend."

"She ... was ... a ... club ... whore."

Pussy smiled. "She was *our* club whore."

Using the butt of his gun, he struck out at the man, slamming the gun down. Over and over he struck Homer until the bastard no longer had a face and he was covered in blood.

No one stopped him. Ronald made to move, but Pussy's brothers fired shots at his feet. When it was over, Pussy went and stood beside Devil, who was covered in as much blood as he was.

"What the fuck does this prove?" Frederick asked.

"Nothing."

"I'm going to ruin you."

"Good." Devil looked toward Snake and nodded.

Snaked pressed a button, and the building behind them started to crumble to the ground.

Frederick looked behind him. "What the fuck are you doing?"

"You take my livelihood, I'll take from you."

"There were people in there." The other man was yelling. He no longer looked like the calm Italian mobster.

"Were there? Ashley was one of mine. So are Death and Curse. Consider this payback."

Devil stepped up close toward Frederick, glaring at the man in the eye.

Pussy stared at his boss. He looked larger, taller, and far more powerful than Frederick.

"You kill me and everyone you love dies," Frederick said.

"I'm not going to kill you. I figured you're the type of coward who'd have shit like that in place. You proved that with Tate and Murphy. They don't wake up and you're going to have Tiny on your case."

"I'm going to own all of you."

Devil chuckled. "No, you're not."

"You can't win this."

"And neither can you. You fuck with me, and I'll fuck with you. This," Devil pointed toward Homer and Kenneth, "is just the start. I can make this worse. I can find every business you ever owned and have it in the ground within hours."

Frederick's rage was clear for them all to see.

"I will win this. You'll die."

"I know, but here's the thing, Fred. I don't give a fuck about dying. Do you? You walk around with your guards and your deals. If someone gets hurt, you hurt someone else. You're afraid to die. I'm not, and I'll take you down with me." Devil continued to stare at Frederick. "Do your own fucking runs from now on. I'm out."

"You owe me."

"And you took one of my women from me. I don't owe you shit. Consider the fact I'm giving you your life and walk the fuck away." Devil stepped away, and they all lowered their weapons. Ronald made no move to reach for his.

Climbing on the back of his bike, Pussy gunned the engine and headed back to the clubhouse with Devil.

Life was going to change, he had no doubt, but he also knew he was going to be living his life with Sasha.

Once they were back at the clubhouse, Lexie didn't say a word as she led Devil away. No words were needed. Pussy took Sasha into the bathroom with him, but he made sure to wash the blood away before she touched him. He wasn't going to risk anything happening to her.

****

Two weeks later

Sasha stood within the doorway. She ran her hand up and down the frame getting used to the feel and texture. Using her walking stick, she ran it around in the room. Pussy had been teaching her the layout of the room, but he was out for the moment and she always practiced when she was alone.

It had been two weeks since Devil had gone to pick a fight. Within the last couple of weeks a lot had happened. Pussy had moved her out of the clubhouse and brought her here. It was a small house near the town center with a small garden. Every day he took her out, counting the steps and helping her get used to where things were. It was nice not having to panic in case she smashed anything. Pussy promised her there were no valuable items around the house.

This was her time to get used to her life. During the day he helped her to become more independent, and by night he taught her exactly why he got his name. Shane, or Pussy, was addicted to licking her out. He spent more time licking her clit than he did fucking her. She did love sucking his cock and hearing him splinter apart underneath her touch. The sounds he made turned her on more.

"Okay, Sasha, you can do this."

Releasing the wall she took three steps into the room. She imagined Pussy behind her. He'd wrap his hand around her waist and whisper the steps.

"Turn left and make one step, turn front and three more." She paused as she recalled where everything was. "Lean forward and there is the coffee table." She felt the coffee table, giggling. "Three steps to the side and sit down." Sasha followed the orders and lowered herself into the chair.

Her achievement was great, and she giggled, clapping her hands.

"Baby, I told you that you could do it," Pussy said. His voice came from behind her.

"I didn't hear you come in."

"I've got you a gift."

"A gift?" What could he have given her? Pussy had gotten her more than enough. The time he spent with her giving her back what Kenneth had taken was more than she could have imagined.

"Stay where you are," he said.

She strained to listen to all the sounds.

"Put your hands out."

She did as he asked, and she encountered fur.

"A dog, you've bought me a dog?" she asked.

"Yes. She's designed to help you. There's going to be a woman come around later to talk you through the commands. You've got to name her though."

Sasha stroked the dog, loving her pet instantly.

"I'm going to name her Ashley, after your friend. She helped to guide you."

Pussy cupped her face and kissed her.

In the last two weeks Pussy had arranged for a proper burial for Ashley. She'd been by his side as Pussy and the rest of the Chaos bleeds crew said their goodbyes to the woman who'd lost her life too soon.

"Fuck, baby, I love you."

She smiled. "I love you. I love you so much."

"You can't ever leave me. Sasha, you've got a pussy I love licking, and I love being around you. You're not getting rid of me any time soon." He dropped a kiss to her temple. "You're stuck with me."

Wrapping her arms around him, she smiled.

Being stuck with Pussy was the best feeling in the world.

Epilogue

Six months later

Somewhere out of Fort Wills

"Butch, wake up, baby, please, you've got to wake up. You can't die," Cheryl said, screaming his name. There was blood everywhere, and none of The Skulls agreed to help him. Everything had gone wrong, and she didn't know how to make it all right. "Please, somebody, help me."

Tiny, Devil, Alex stared down at the body refusing to help. Why wouldn't they help? Butch had done everything they asked.

He didn't tell you about the Savage Brothers MC.

"He's dead. Leave him be," Tiny said, spitting on the ground. He was covered in blood, his arm holding a giant gash that revealed too much of his flesh. Gonzalez and the Savage Brothers had taken them all by surprise, and now both crews were having to pay the price.

"No, he's not dead. I can feel a pulse. Please, you've got to help him." Cheryl tried to cover the bullet wound to keep his blood from leaving his body.

No one was helping. Sandy was passing out across the room. What remained of the Fort Wills town hall left a lot to be desired. Civilians were running around trying to get away from the attack that had fallen on the town within days of Tiny going to war with Devil. For the first time in years Devil and Tiny didn't get along. They'd all been mistaken. Gonzalez never intended to choose between the two men. He was going to take on Fort Wills and Piston County, killing all of them. Cheryl saw the glares they were shooting at her man. It was all a big mistake. They were all staring at Butch as if he was a rat, vermin, something they couldn't bring themselves to touch. Didn't they know he was helping them all?

"He's not getting my fucking help," Zero said, standing up. "He's fucking dead to me."

"This is what Gonzalez wants," she said. Butch had told her everything about what he'd done and why. Gonzalez had to be put down. There was no way to stop what he had to do. He was betraying his brothers, and yet he was protecting them at the same time. The Savage Brothers was in his blood. He was helping all three clubs without even picking one. The Skulls were his home.

Butch did what Alex told him to. He told her everything, not leaving anything out. The Skulls and Chaos Bleeds were refusing to see the truth, and now the love of her life was dying in her arms. Glancing around the room, she saw members of both crews were dying all around them.

She tried to think fast.

Staring at one man to the other, she tried to figure out the fastest way to help her man.

All of them, apart from Alex, were married. Those women were in a safe house, or at least they thought it was safe. Butch arranged for the women and children to be at the warehouse in the hope of luring Gonzalez away from them. The Savage Brothers knew where they were and perhaps Gonzalez did as well.

"If you let Butch die, every single person you hold dear will die," she said, letting her words sink in.

"They're safe."

"Are they? Have you heard from Lexie? Eva? Tate? They're all where Butch put them, and I know I can end their lives if his heart stops beating." She gritted her teeth as the blood seeped through her fingers.

Cheryl was willing to do everything to save her man even put the lives of the clubs' women at stake.

The End

www.samcrescent.com

SAM CRESCENT

EVERNIGHT PUBLISHING ®

www.evernightpublishing.com

www.ingramcontent.com/pod-product-compliance
Lightning Source LLC
Chambersburg PA
CBHW022128170626
46808CB00002B/900